REMNANTS OF THE SUN

J.A. Day

Remnants Of The Sun by J.A. Day
jadaybooks.com
Copyright © 2021 J.A. Day
Cover Art by Meli Kovacs.
Cover Art Copyright © 2021 Meli Kovacs

All rights reserved. No portion of this book may be reproduced in any form without permission from the publisher, except as permitted by copyright law. For permissions contact james@jadaybooks.com

In memory of Emily Perugia
I'm Sure You're Having Fun In Paradise

Part One

New Pieces

THE BEST WAY TO CHANGE THINGS IS TO GET THE KING DRUNK AND FED. THEN YOU TELL HIM WHAT YOU NEED

'Diary of the King's Skald' by Alf Beumers

Sigrun hadn't been invited to the feast but she attended anyway. This was the exclusive get together where all the important family members of the wagon train met. She had to be here to finally make a difference to her life.

A lowly cattle rancher like her was not meant to find this kind of party. The prominent sons, daughters, nieces, and nephews, and grand-children of the three family Elders did not discuss important decisions with the lowly workers. They had tried to hide the feast well, but Sigrun had spent all evening checking the sides of wagons for any tell-tale runes, or searching in the darkening sky for any sign of a fire. Eventually she found the feast in a small square, made by a dozen or so wagons.

The guard, a tall man with long wavy hair and gaunt cheekbones, gave her a suspicious look. He clearly knew she wasn't meant to be there because of her faded tunic with many holes in the fabric, and trousers with mud at the cuffs. Undeterred, Sigrun kept herself straight and strode up to the guard. "Sven Baldur said I was invited."

"Oh yeah, he let any random woman with dirt on her trousers in?" the guard said, narrowing his eyes. "Are you just here to serve drinks, or are you the after-feast entertainment?"

Sigrun had been to enough parties to know what kind of entertainment the guard was talking about. She rolled her eyes, and acted annoyed – not hard with the way this man was behaving.

"You might want to watch what you say to me. If I tell Sven you have been rude you will be cleaning up horse shit for a week."

"You're clearly not meant to be here, lady. Run along," the guard said, shooing her with his hand.

She stepped up to him, nose nearly touching his face. Her heart pounded, but she wasn't afraid to be in a fight. In her teenage years Sigrun had taught herself how to brawl, and how to use a sword. Besides, the best way to prove that you were meant to be at this feast was to be annoyed at anyone blocking your way and to not back down if they did.

"Go get Sven, or we'll see whose the lady," she growled.

The guard stared at her for a moment, probably weighing up if a fight was worth it. He harrumphed, turned around, and disappeared behind the wagons. Sigrun smiled.

Now she had to hope that Sven Baldur recognized her, and agree to let her in.

Sven Baldur was the son of Gregor, who ran the farmers in the wagon train. Sven was tipped to lead everything when Gregor died, but he didn't act like he was important. He liked to dance and drink with the common people. That was how Sigrun met him. A few weeks ago he was at a party, sat at a table. Sigrun sat opposite and introduced herself. It didn't take long for them to hit it off, and that night the conversation and drink flowed. Her memory of what exactly they talked about was fuzzy, but she did remember Sven told her to come see him sometime. She was going to use that promise right here and now to gain an invite to this feast.

The guard came back with Sven in tow. He had the black hair and thick arms that were common among the Baldur's. His face was round and small. Sven always had a smile, but his eyes had a steely seriousness to them. He examined Sigrun.

She wanted to say something, try to plead why

she should be let in. She might be a lowly cattle rancher that didn't matter too much to the wagon train overall, but she was here to change that and prove to them that she could do more with her life. If they gave her a chance to lead or make decisions, they would find that the people under her would be more passionate about their jobs or the decisions would be better thought through. But she couldn't say any of that because it would reveal that she wasn't really meant to be here. This would make it highly likely they would grab her and drag her back to the edges of the wagon train.

So instead she gave the guard and Sven a hard and annoyed stare with her fierce eyes. She raised her strong jawline up, trying to appear like she was above them. "You told me I was invited."

Sven tittered as he examined her, which didn't seem good. Sigrun tensed up, ready to stand her ground if they tried to grab her. But to her surprise he said, "She's invited," and waved her through.

The guard was just as surprised, and he bowed an apology. But when Sigrun walked past he gave her one last narrow eyed stare, which she reciprocated.

The guard went completely out of her mind when she stepped into the square.

Smoke from the various bonfires filled Sigrun's lungs. When she got past the haze she found the wagon train's distinguished leaders sat at one long table. The men wore smart tunics, while the women wore flowing dresses. They both wore navy or green cloaks, fastened with silver brooches, family runes glittering in the firelight.

She strode towards the table. But the more she saw the fine clothes and noble manners and compared them to her faded tunic and drunken past the more unsure she became. Why did she think she could sit amongst these well dressed people and charm them enough to be granted a more important job? What could she say to them that they would be interested in or laugh at? All her knowledge was in herding cows and getting drunk. She was sure those subjects would go down well with people who have read books from different cultures, and knew things about the world or politics.

For a second she wanted to abandon her plan, turn around, and drink whiskey back at her wagon. But she chided that instinct. She was here to do something important with her life, to stop wasting it away by getting blind drunk every week.

To calm her nerves of having to meet and talk to her betters, she grabbed the long braid at the back of her blond hair and felt the contours of its knots. She had been taught how to tie the knots by her mother, and every time she touched them she was transported back to the lesson and her mother's soothing voice. She had told Sigrun that she could do anything, if she worked at it.

A few young women carried plates with tankards of beer around the table. When Sigrun walked past she took two, wanting to feel confident when she talked to the important family members. She gulped half the bitter liquid down.

Sigrun sat at the middle of the table with Sven. The Baldurs around him gave her a curious glance. She drank some more, and dismissed the self conscious thoughts that told her she was not dressed properly for the occasion. She couldn't do anything about how she was dressed – literally these were the best clothes she had in the wardrobe – but she could do something about the way she acted. And she was going to act as charming and as funny as she could.

"Sorry about the way I'm clothed, I slipped in the mud several times when coming here."

There were a few titters from the Baldurs, and when Sven chuckled there seemed to be an air of relief and acceptance amongst the group.

Sigrun looked around the table to see who she could start a conversation with. Sven leant into his buddy's ear, whispering something. He wasn't the best way to start a conversation. The men next to her were shouting boisterously about whose farmers would harvest the most produce in the season. It wasn't exactly a competition she could claim any participation in. She eyed a woman opposite in a gray dress who was talking with a young man.

The woman had black brushed back hair and hawk eyes. She was quite attractive in an austere and stern way. For a second Sigrun grinned at the thought of having sex with the daughter or niece of a Baldur, but she reminded herself that this wasn't a normal party. Wasn't she supposed to be done with meaningless sex?

She drank some more, and made sure to listen to what the gray dressed woman and the young man were talking about.

"Do you think the Mattsons will punish us by

refusing us meat like they did Gregor and Yael?" the woman asked.

The young man, who had blond hair and a sharp nose, glanced down the table. "I don't get why we still invite them. It's not like Rita is going to appear."

Sigrun followed the blond man's gaze and sure enough at the end of the table sat a few Mattsons. She could tell by their distinctive red hair and freckles. The seats between their group and the Baldurs were empty, like either family wanted as much space between the other as possible.

So the rumors about a split between the Mattsons and Baldurs were true. She had heard people in previous parties talking about it, but details about what had happened and why were scant. This feast was the perfect place to get the real story, but outright asking would show Sigrun to be the outsider she was. The guests would know that she was not meant to be there and would probably ignore her for the rest of the evening. She had to try to get the answer more subtly.

"I've had many butchers convincing me to give them more of my cows," she said loudly to the two sat opposite. "Are they trying to hoard all the meat or something?"

The woman in the gray dress glanced at her. "It's for the weekly parties which Jarl Hannes is throwing. You have to have a feast every weekend, apparently."

Ah so that was she had gone to more parties in the last few months than she had in her lifetime. The dances and feasts were usually an every month or season kind of thing, but ever since Hannes was named Jarl they had become a weekly occurrence.

The young blond man took a swig of his drink. "Gregor was furious when he found out how much food was being used. That was why he and Yael voted him out."

Sigrun nodded, sipping her beer. She felt like she was only getting a bare summary of the politics in the wagon train. What the blond man said didn't explain why the relationship between the Mattsons and the Baldurs was so frosty. But before she could ask for more details, the gray dressed woman turned back to her companion.

"So how are you going to be different from Hannes then?"

"By not pissing off your uncle for one," the blond man said.

Clearly they were trying to ignore her, so

Sigrun sat back and drank more of her beer.

She looked around the table for any more conversations to join. Every Baldur talked with their neighbor, and there didn't appear to be any gaps she could fit her way in. At the Mattson end it looked quiet, but if she sat with them she would be making a political statement that would not be liked by most who attended this feast, including Sven. And she couldn't jeopardize even the casual relationship she had with Sven, it had got her into this feast after all. At the other end of the table were men and women with the distinct chubby look of the Hoademakers, who ran the weavers and the handymen. Everyone sat prim and proper, and sipped their drinks. Their conversations weren't as intense or unbreakable as the Baldurs, so Sigrun decided that she would walk over and see if she could get any more information about Hannes and the Elders, or even just a drinking buddy.

But as soon as Sigrun stood up, everyone at the table stood up as well. She was a little confused, but then saw two figures appear through the bonfire smoke. They were two of the most important Elders in the wagon train, progenitors of most of the people who sat around this table: Yael Hoademaker and Gregor Baldur.

Yael was thin and trim for someone in his family, though his face had the familiar Hoademaker chubbiness. He wore a black cloak that went down to his legs, and underneath the thinnest and finest tunic Sigrun had ever seen. He hobbled instead of walked, resting his hand on a long black cane, which had a silver spinning wheel on the top. Gregor was short, wide, and had thick muscular arms. He had a bushy black beard, which he twisted and knotted into braids. On his neck was a silver necklace with a pendant depicting a shining Sol.

The two Elders motioned for them to sit. As Sigrun did she drank several gulps of her beer. Her heart pounded like mad, and she felt a little sick. She had been prepared to meet important family members within the wagon train and talk to them, she hadn't been prepared to meet two family Elders. One wrong word or a casual insult could be disastrous. She had heard rumors that if you were really disliked by the Elders you would be exiled.

She felt another urge to run out of the square. Her brain buzzed, and the stars in the sky brightened and blurred across the sky. She had drunk too much already, which would increase the chances of making a fool of herself.

But how many times would she get an opportunity to meet and talk with the Elders? If anyone was going to give her a job where she could make decisions or make a difference it would definitely be them. If she could impress them her plan for tonight would have succeeded beyond her wildest dreams. She had to stay.

Yael hobbled towards the Mattson end of the table, while Gregor sat with the Hoademakers. The talk around Sigrun sounded louder and more excited. It appeared that the important family members had expected this visit to happen, talking about what they were going to say to impress the two Elders. From what Sigrun could gather, Yael and Gregor were going to decide on a very important matter, but the details of what eluded her.

At the Mattson end of the table, the talk with Yael didn't go well. She couldn't hear anything but the faces of the Mattsons had a look of disbelief or rage. Yael put up his hands to try to calm the situation down, but one Mattson shook his head and pushed himself up. Soon the others followed suit.

"You should be making amends with Hannes, not choosing someone else," said the Mattson who had stood up.

Yael said something that Sigrun couldn't hear. The Mattson didn't find it persuasive. He shook his head again and stormed off. The others followed. Yael gave one last grimace their way, before pushing up from his cane and hobbling down the table.

The Hoademakers were usually known for trying to keep the peace within the wagon train. There was a big divide between the faithful side and the workers' side. The Mattsons hated the faith with a passion, but the Baldurs had always been close with the faith. They had been the first outside faith family to join the wagon train, but a lot of their members married or joined the faith down the years. However nowadays the farmers that the Baldurs led were starting to break away from that. The faith had become very preachy when it came to what they considered shadow, targeting the parties the people liked going to and shouting about the dangers of drinking, overeating, and having casual sex. No one seemed to like this more purity based direction. The Mattsons convinced the farmers to join them in protesting against the faith, but Gregor and his family still wouldn't go against their old allies. So it was a surprise to see Elder Hoademaker, Yael, on the same side as Gregor in terms of going against the Mattsons. He usually liked to go with the direction that would cause the least resistance. What was he gaining from going against that instinct?

Gregor looked to be having a long conversation with a few of the Hoademakers. A lot of the chubby faces looked excited and passionate about what they were telling him. Gregor didn't look persuaded with anything they were saying, looking stern as usual. When the Hoademakers finished, he just gave a curt nod and stood up, walking down and taking a seat next to the blond man. Yael sat opposite Sven and his companion.

Sigrun wondered who she was going to talk to and what she was going to say. She wished she knew what the two Elders were here for. From the talk about Hannes, it definitely felt connected to the Jarl in some way. She felt she needed more information, so she leaned forwards to hear the conversation between Gregor and the blond haired man.

"What would you do if you had the power?" Gregor said, staring intently.

"I'd trade more with the towns and cities. We produce great food, and we have found some good mines that haven't been claimed around the area," the blond haired man said.

"Wouldn't trading food exacerbate our consumption problems?"

The blond haired man widened his eyes, and squeezed his hand. "Shit...but I think the mine thing can still work."

Gregor fiddled with the braids in his beard. "I'll think about it."

He turned towards the gray dressed woman. The blond haired man looked crushed, he had just lost his chance.

Sigrun found the whole exchange fascinating. Why had Gregor been asking the power question? What kind of answer was he and Yael wanting, and what would they do with the answer? But before Sigrun could figure it out, Yael's cane hit the ground in front of her, and the Hoademaker Elder shook and grimaced while he sat down opposite.

"I don't think I'm aware of you," Yael said, examining her.

"You wouldn't be, I'm just a cattle rancher that looks after cows," she said, feeling as small and insignificant as her job role implied.

"Interesting that Sven would choose someone

outside of the family to be here. But we will see what you have to offer."

Yael's stare made her feel uncomfortable. It was like he was scrutinizing her, judging her. She felt her stomach roil, and for a moment she didn't know what to say, fearing she would throw up on the food. This was her moment, she couldn't screw it up.

Yael leant forwards, gripping the cane's silver spinning wheel. "So, what would you do with the power of the Jarl?"

Sigrun finally put everything about the party in place: the excitement, the talk about Hannes, the anger the Mattsons displayed, and the fact that two Elders were here. This feast was to choose who would be the next Jarl.

This revelation brought a mixture of feelings within her. One of them was excitement, she wouldn't just get the opportunity to be one of the important people in the wagon train, she would be the most important person in the wagon train. Only the Keeper of the Sol Shard, the head of the faith, had as much power as the Jarl did. They could decide where the wagon train went, who they traded with, and what laws were brought in. The other feeling was absolute terror, because she would curse herself all her life if she screwed this encounter up.

However, she had an advantage. She knew exactly how to answer Yael's question. "With the power of the Jarl I'd find a goal for the workers to have of their own."

"What do you mean? Our goal is to grow food, cook that food, make clothes, and fix the wagons when needed," Yael said.

"Yes, but what is that in service of? It is in service of the Mission of Sol. This is the faith's wagon train, and we follow them because they want to proselytize to the world to bring back their dead sun. But a lot of the workers don't really believe in that. I want to explore the world to find out about its history, Edven down the way wants to find some nice pasture to grow old in, and many of the farmers I've spoken to at parties just want to be stationary and tend to a proper land of their own."

"We have always been a nomadic tribe, that's what people signed up for," Yael said, leaning forwards. "Besides, it's not like it's a prison. The people who want to settle down can always do so when we visit a town or city."

"That's what their great grandfathers signed up

for, not them," Sigrun said, feeling excited about being able to talk to someone about this. "And people can't just easily settle down even if they want to. They have friends here, family members, a community they are a part of. Not to mention the fact that this wagon train gives them more freedom and power than they might in some towns. We have been to a few where the workers are pretty much slaves."

"You're saying that we should all settle down somewhere? The Mission would not allow that for a second, they believe in their faith with zeal. It's the reason why the workers have gone cold towards them. And it's not like we have two Sol Shards."

Sigrun nodded. "You're right, we can't easily split. Unlike raiders we can't live out in the icy world without a Sol Shard. But previous Jarls have never really thought about solutions that could work, all they try to gain is power within the system. But the system is always going to be on the Mission's side, they do have the weapons and the Sol Shard."

"There's always taking over," Yael said, grimacing.

"Too bloody, and it would take a lot of training

for farmers and weavers to get to the same level of swordsmanship a Priestess and Priest has."

Yael shifted in his seat, looking uncomfortable. He rubbed his cane, letting silence fill the table. It was at that point that Sigrun realized that everyone at the feast wasn't talking anymore. Most of the people that surrounded them were listening in on their conversation. Gregor stood behind Yael, finished with his talks.

Sigrun could feel the hatred coming from the other people staring at her. They seemed to ask, "who are you to be talking about this stuff?" There was a part of her that agreed with that assessment. She was nobody really, just some woman that had spent a lot of time thinking about these things because she didn't like the way things were going with her life, and she had decided that changing the system would improve her own life as well.

Yael glanced around. "Hmm we seem to have gotten an audience. Well, last question, what are the solutions you feel could work?"

Sigrun sipped her drink, calming her nerves. "There are two solutions I see: convince the Mission that the majority of people in the wagon train want to settle down and they should follow that, or convince them to go out into the world and find another Sol Shard so the people who want to settle down can."

"And you think we could convince them of either of those?"

"I think the first one would be very hard, but the second one might be doable. I heard a rumor that the current Keeper has died, and who knows who the next one is going to be. They could be more reasonable."

Yael furrowed his brow. He gripped the spinning wheel on his cane, pushed himself up, and turned around to Gregor. While the two Elders whispered to one another, everyone on the table sat and stared at Sigrun in silence. She had no idea whether what was happening was good or bad. All she could do was sip her beer and wave at the people looking at her.

The talk between Yael and Gregor seemed animated. Yael was gesturing a lot with his non cane hand. Gregor looked skeptical, and pointed to the woman in the gray dress and one of the Hoademakers. Yael shook his head and pointed back to Sigrun. Gregor rubbed his braids, and mouthed, "Are you sure?" Yael nodded.

The Elder Hoademaker turned around, putting

up his hands to the men and women sitting at the table. "We have come to a decision. The person we are naming Jarl, actually I don't know her name." He stepped towards Sigrun, and asked. "What's your name?"

"Sigrun," she said, shocked at what was happening. Were they really giving her the Jarl job?

"Yes, the person we are naming as the next Jarl is Sigrun."

Many at the table gasped, including Sigrun herself. This couldn't be real. This had to be a joke. All she wanted from going to the feast was to get to know the important family members of the wagon train, maybe at most get some low level job from one of them. She had definitely not expected at the end of the night to be named Jarl.

But the clap of her back, and the handshake from both Yael and Gregor didn't feel like a joke. And Gregor wasn't known to be the type to play practical jokes. His son Sven was, but Gregor certainly wasn't.

Sigrun still felt disbelief, still internalized the narrowed eyed stares that told her she didn't deserve this. But there was a part of her that felt pure joy from the announcement. Jarl Sigrun, hey, that was a name that was going to be written in the history books.

AFTER YOU DIE YOUR SOUL GETS TRANSPORTED INTO THE SKY, AND RESIDES IN SOL'S RESTING PLACE

'Scroll of Spirit'

Sonja's mother had died. It happened a few days ago, her mother had just gone to bed after prayers and never woke up again. It was a peaceful death, one many would wish for, but that didn't mean the death didn't cause a massive amount of trauma for everyone in the Mission. For Sonja's mother wasn't just her mother, she was also the Keeper of the Sol Shard, and leader of the Mission of Sol, the faith that founded the wagon train.

Outside the wagon where Sonja's mother rested, there was a whole crowd of faithful waiting for their chance to see the coffin. Sonja and her friends were lucky to get a private viewing because of their special connection to her.

The Keeper wasn't really Sonja's mother, neither was she Roose's, Britta's, or Teresa's. But they felt like she was. The Keeper had saved them all from orphaned lives of misery. She gave them a place within the Mission, cared and taught them personally, and even promoted them to the most important jobs in the faith when they became adults. Their mother meant the most to them, so why couldn't Sonja feel anything about her death?

The wooden coffin had a portrait of the Keeper on top. It was a striking portrait, it showed off her mother's passionate face and wise eyes. It was a big contrast to Sonja herself. Her eyes were always too wide and her face narrow. Her mother had bright blond hair, while Sonja's hair was black

Staring at her mother's wise eyes made her feel nothing. She wasn't sad, she wasn't empty, she wasn't in shock, or numb. She just felt...normal. Like it was just another day of prayers and work.

It was a little awkward not feeling anything Roose, Britta, and Teresa were all bent over with tears, crying about how it was too soon and how they were going to miss their mother. Sonja made sure not to catch their gaze, just so they wouldn't complain about her not showing enough emotion.

Most of Sonja's focus was not on the coffin but on the Sol Shard. The white crystal hung on a golden chain. The crystal glowed inside, a deep orange glow. The glow emanated a protective heat which allowed the people within the wagon train to live in the icy wasteland that the world had become. Sonja could feel the Shard calling to her, like Sol wanted her to touch it.

The value of the crystal didn't just lie in the life it gave, it was also a piece of Sol. A connection to the goddess that used to rule the earth and had made it a paradise full of green grass, trees, and flowers. The Mission, and Sonja, deeply believed that one day Sol would come back to rule the skies, and the people of the earth would all be able to live in that paradise land again. The only way they could do that was to get rid of Manang's influence, his shadow.

Maybe that was why she didn't feel anything for the Keeper, because her heart and mind was too full of shadow. It had been for most of her life.

The shadow had started innocently enough. Sonja had always noticed girls: the way they styled their hair, the way they dressed, the grace in which they walked, and in particular the way their arms moved while fighting with the blade. Sometimes she could stare at another girl quite intently for a few minutes, getting lost in admiration. Unfortunately, she got caught staring during Scroll Class.

She had been staring at Britta, liking her golden curly hair and the way the back of her neck looked. But when Britta turned she noticed Sonja, and gave her a disgusted look. Britta went up to the teacher and told on her. This got Sonja's mother involved.

Sonja was called out of class by the Keeper. She was led to the yellow wood pews placed in rows outside the Keeper's wagon. The Keeper sat, and patted the space next to her for Sonja to sit.

Sonja's heart pounded, She rubbed her hands, and didn't want to look her mother in the eye. Sonja didn't know what she had done wrong, but she knew it must be something big.

"Why do you think you were staring at that girl?" her mother asked.

"Have I done something wrong?" she said, feeling her stomach roil.

"That really depends on the answer that you give."

Sonja had no idea what answer her mother wanted. What was so wrong with staring at Britta in the way she had? She just shook her head.

"Do you think it has anything to do with being gay? You know how we forbid that," The Keeper said.

She looked up at her, surprised at the statement. Her mother's face looked stern, the question was a serious one.

At that moment she didn't understand how what she was doing could be connected to being gay. She was only staring at other girls, liking...and then it dawned on her.

She had seen some of the older girls look appreciatively at the farmers in the wagon train, and heard them talk about the way they worked or the look of their muscular arms. She had been looking at girls and appreciating them in the same way.

And then the second thing her mother had said hit her: it was forbidden. If she told the Keeper what she wanted deep down was the love of another woman then the Keeper would have no choice but to exile her from the Mission. Maybe her mother would even send her back to the workhouse, where hundreds of children slept on dirty floors, and the adults made them work until they exhausted themselves to death. She couldn't go back there, couldn't be chucked out of the Mission that had given her a purpose in life. So she lied.

"I guess I was staring at Britta because I admire the way she goes about learning the scrolls, but I understand now that it disturbs her, and others around me. I will make sure to not let it happen again."

The Keeper examined her, a stare that felt like it dug in and exposed her. Did her mother know she was lying, could she suspect what staring at Britta truly meant?

"And you're sure this won't happen again?"

Sonja bowed her head. "I make a solemn promise, Keeper."

Her mother squeezed her shoulder. "Good, now run along back to class."

But those desires could not be so easily held back, especially as Sonja got older. The desires became more burning, more urgent. She didn't just want to stare at other women, she wanted to kiss them, touch them, and she wanted them to touch her.

The burning desire got so bad one evening that she couldn't sleep. She just wanted someone, anyone, to fulfil her desire. And it couldn't just be herself, that wasn't enough, plus it was hard to do when she slept in a room full of bunk beds with other Priestesses in.

Sonja decided she had enough and tiptoed out of the wagon. Avoiding the guard on patrol, she went out of the Mission's encampment and into the wider wagon train.

Every follower of the faith knew that people within the wagon train held parties full of drinking, feasting, and casual sex. There was a game that some Priestesses would play about who could devise the worst punishment to the people who went to these parties, or what the most sordid thing was happening within them. In one of these games Roose had told them that she knew how to find the parties, that they needed to follow certain runes and randomly placed bits of furniture within the wagon train. Many Priestesses thought she was having them on.

But when Sonja went out into the darkness of the wagon train that night, she actually found small runes painted on the sides of wagons, which led her down streets where random pieces of furniture were placed in odd directions, following these eventually led her towards a party.

She found a small grassy square, full of tables with food and drink. People danced around bonfires, grinding against each other in very sexual ways. The smoke of the bonfires quickly filled her lungs, and the smell of roasting pork or beef made her hungry. Everything happening within the party was against what the faith taught, but at that moment, with what she was feeling, she didn't care.

Sonja didn't know how long she danced and drank for, but she felt good just letting go. Eventually, another woman caught her eye, this one had long blond hair and strong arms. She decided to go up to her for a chat. The chat became flirtatious, and the flirting became a burning desire to go back to her wagon, which Sonja did.

It was only when she woke up that Sonja felt regret and shame. She had gone against her teachings in a big way. She had committed many shadows, the worst one being same sex love. Sonja snuck out of the blond woman's wagon, feeling a loathing within herself.

She felt like she needed to be punished. She would tell her mother that she had committed this grave shadow, but when she thought about it a flash came into her mind of being dragged out of the wagon train and into the workhouse. There she would be whipped and beaten until she couldn't take it anymore. Even though that punishment may be what she deserved, she felt a paralyzing fear of having to experience it.

If she decided then and there to forget what

she had done, and make an effort to be purer next time then surely she could be forgiven by Sol?

But the purity didn't last. Every few weeks she would have the burning desire again, and she would wander towards those parties. It didn't even stop with just the wagon train. Whenever the caravan got to a new town or city, she would sneak into it and sample the kind of parties and women they had.

But just like the first time, after every occasion she gave in she hated herself and wanted to punish herself. Sonja always vowed to be purer next time.

This oscillation between desire and shame made Sonja feel more and more miserable being part of the faith. Even though she was going up the ranks, being made Priestess when she was fifteen – one of the youngest ever – and then being promoted to General in her twenties, she felt an emptiness inside, and drifted away from the teachings.

In her moments of desire she didn't understand why the Mission was so against all the things she was doing, it made her feel so good and happy. But when she was in her purity moments she got frustrated how others didn't follow the teachings as strictly or as purely as her. Wasn't their Mission supposed to be convincing others to follow their example. If no one did, what was the point of proselytizing to them?

Now her mother was dead. A mother that hadn't known any of this, couldn't know any of it because otherwise she would have exiled her long ago.

But now Sonja was an adult she understood the fears about being exiled to the workhouse were unfounded. Nowadays, the workers' side of the wagon train was more and more separate from the faith. Maybe now that the Keeper was dead she should admit to herself what she truly was. Maybe she should quit the faith and be the person that she wanted to be: someone open with who they loved and didn't care about anyone else's opinion on it.

Sonja put her hand on the coffin. She stared at the portrait of her mother, mouthing goodbye. She would tell her friends, and the Mission, that she was quitting after the Quartermaster let them know her mother's final wishes.

Every faithful was there at the final wishes speech. Priests and Priestess sat shoulder to shoulder on the yellow wood pews, while Acolytes had to stand at the back. There were also a surprising amount of non-dedicated faithful. At the sides of the pews stood many Baldurs, including Gregor Baldur himself. Even though the Baldur side of the caravan was supposed to be one with the faith, they very rarely came to prayers or events anymore.

The sky above was thick with clouds, and a light rain pattered down on the heads of the gathered, but many were too excited to be bothered by this.

Sonja sat at the front, along with her friends: Roose, Britta, and Teresa. Sonja could feel the stares at the back of her head. She heard whispers amongst the gathered, gossiping about which one of her group would be the new Keeper.

When her mother had died she had not designated an heir to the title of Keeper. This was unusual, a Keeper usually liked to name a successor a few years before they were likely to die - to keep the transition of power smooth. And her mother had been known to be wise when it came to these kinds of decisions, which made people question why there had been such an oversight.

Everyone knew it would be one of her "children", but which one of the four would be chosen changed with the cold winds. Some said Sonja, others said Britta, one season Roose was the favorite, and a few weeks Teresa was named. There would also be periods of time when rumors said the Keeper hadn't chosen yet because none of them were worthy enough.

Sonja hated the attention of these rumors. She knew that she wouldn't be chosen as the new Keeper. In the last few years she had barely talked to her mother, apart from a few words about new patrols or where they could travel to avoid raiders. Every time they did talk there had been frostiness in the air, both wanting to get the talk over with as soon as possible.

And Sonja was perfectly fine with that. Not just because she had finally decided to leave the Mission, but because she knew she probably wouldn't make a good Keeper. She was too full of shadow and she had deep dislike with the purity angle the faith taught. She wouldn't be able to handle the responsibility of the whole religion without messing it up.

The Quartermaster, a thin man with black hair named Sigmund, stepped onto the platform that jutted out of the Keeper's wagon. The platform held a lectern, which he unrolled a scroll onto. Everyone leant forward and held their breath as he started to speak.

However, they quickly let it out again and slumped in their chair when Sigmund only mentioned the small gifts the Keeper was handing out. A few of the Priests and Priestesses bowed as their names and items were called out, but it was obvious that they didn't really care about this and they just wanted the Quartermaster to get to who the next Keeper was going to be.

Even though they probably knew they wouldn't get it, Sonja still saw faces of hope amongst the Priests and Priestesses. They still held onto the rumors that her, Roose, Britta, or Teresa wasn't good enough and the Keeper might say someone else. It made her feel uncomfortable. The people in the faith wanted power a little too readily in her eyes. The scrolls didn't exactly say ambition was a shadow, but she felt that they came close to saying it.

The scroll reading came to a part where the Keeper said names of men and women that should be commended and would receive a special medal or title. Many in the rows behind Sonja started to fidget and yawn, making her a little annoyed. Did they not have respect for their leader, were they really only here to know who the next leader was going to be? She thought they should be more cut up about the loss of her mother, but then again she hadn't felt anything either. Could she really judge them for something she didn't feel?

Thankfully, it looked like the Quartermaster was getting to the end. People started to pay attention again, and held their breath.

"My final act of Keeper is one of naming my successor," Sigmund said, the pews getting very quiet. "I name the new Keeper: Sonja."

Many in the crowd let out groans, sighs, or shouts of "I knew it."

All except Sonja herself. She was stunned that her name had been read out. If any of the four were going to get the title, it should have been Britta.

Britta had the passion and the commitment for the faith. She had always been the Keeper's right hand woman, and always made sure to bring the teaching of the scrolls in line with their mother's view of things. It just didn't make sense for Sonja to be named, and she could see on Britta's face that her sister knew it.

Everyone in the space stared at her, even the Quartermaster. They all expected her to go up on the platform and make a speech. They wanted to know straight away how different or the same she was going to be as Keeper.

She felt all those eyes bore into her, judging her. She couldn't deal with them, she had no plan for being Keeper. Just a moment ago she was ready to quit the faith…and now this?

Her chest felt tight and she struggled to breathe. She had to get out.

Ignoring the cries of surprise or shock, Sonja ran away from the congregation, out of the faith enclosure. She wanted to get lost amongst the maze of wagons.

THE WEIGHT OF THE WORLD ON YOUR SHOULDERS, THE KNOWLEDGE THAT EVERY DECISION YOU MAKE COULD KILL OR HARM PEOPLE, WHY WOULD ANYONE WANT THAT KIND OF POWER?

'The Unhappy King' by Lysanne Lungbourg

Sigrun's mouth was dry and her head throbbed, but it wasn't as bad a wake up as usual. Usually the morning after a party she would be throwing off the covers and running outside to be sick on the grass. This morning she only felt a slight discomfort in her stomach and a need for water. It seemed she was improving.

Had the party last night been real? In the light that was streaming through the gaps in the wagon's slats, the events of what happened felt like a dream. She had been within a table of important people, she had spoken to Yael Hoademaker, and both him and Gregor had made her the Jarl. If any other cattle rancher had told her that story she would have told them to lay off the whiskey. And here she was back in her own wagon, usually in the fables the person that had just become the princess found herself in a magnificent castle and woke up to a handsome prince – not that she would want to wake up to a handsome prince, she was more into princesses.

Sigrun pulled away the covers, and stood up. She felt the roughness of the wood, still the same rickety, splintered planks. She walked to the wardrobe and peered inside, still the same faded and muddy clothes. She brushed her hand into her mess of blond hair and felt the knots of her braid, still the same Sigrun. Nothing was different, and yet why did she have memories that she had been named the most important person in the wagon train?

There was a knock at her door. Sigrun didn't usually get visitors. The cattle ranchers were usually a solitary bunch, tending to their own cows and not disturbing others. On rare occasions they sometimes spent the evening drinking, but usually they would ask you first. Who could be at her door? She opened it and found that it was Sven.

Outside, the bright red light of Manang's blood eye shone down, painting the sky red. Sven stood in the doorway, looking amused but his eyes kept their steely quality.

He glanced up and down at her. "You might

want to get dressed, you were wearing those clothes last night."

It did look like she was wearing the same faded tunic and muddy trousers as she wore at the party, seemingly she had not changed before getting into bed. That at least felt like the aftermath of a normal night out.

"What are you doing here?" she asked.

"I'm here to give you a tour of your new kingdom," he said, mock bowing. "I'm your new adviser."

"So last night wasn't a dream?"

"If it is then we are all participating in it."

Sigrun furrowed her brow, feeling the sense of fear and joy that she had last night when being named Jarl. She nodded, and closed the door.

If this was going to be her first day then she would have to wear something special for the occasion. Unfortunately, the quality of her clothes still hadn't changed. All her choices were ones of various different levels of mud and grime. She chose the one that seemed to have the least, which because she had chosen similarly last night meant that it had more mud stains than the tunic she was wearing now. Sigrun sighed, surely she could get the Hoademakers to make her some new clothes. She changed into her new tunic and trousers, and opened the door. She stepped down next to Sven.

The sky above slowly gathered dark clouds and thunder boomed in the distance. Thankfully the weather meant she didn't have to feel too guilty about not letting her cows out this morning, though she was sure to get soaked with all the walking within the wagon train they were going to do.

Sven seemed to have the same idea, looking up in the sky and frowning. "I better make this tour quick. We don't want the new Jarl to be absolutely soaked on her first day."

"I'm still unsure how this is all going to work, I mean what is going to happen to my wagon, my cows, my things? Also I have no idea how exactly the political system works. I think you've made a mistake."

Sven chuckled. "Yes, we are pretty good at making those."

Sigrun felt a weight fall in her stomach. So she wasn't being made Jarl, this was all just a joke.

But Sven stopped laughing and patted her on the shoulder. "Sorry, I shouldn't be joking like that. We didn't make a mistake, Yael and Gregor chose you for a reason. As for how it is going to work, I'll tell you but we should get going and visit the sights first."

She still felt unsure, worried that Sven was leading her on with this Jarl business and she would find herself a fool in front of the important family members. But she was curious, and if it was real then Sven was right and they should get going.

Sigrun's wagon, and that of the other cattle ranchers, was located in a field of grass at the edges of the wagon train. This was so the cows could have enough space to graze. It stood a few hundred yards away from the mass of wagons that made up the bulk of the wagon train.

To Sigrun it felt like she was always separated from other people, that she was a lonely other that many didn't see day to day. It wasn't that the wagon train was foreign to her, during the period when the train would first stake its roots in a new place - when the underlying snow was melting so the cows had to stay in their trailer and eat feed - she would find herself wandering through the maze of wagons, meeting people, and attending parties, but it sometimes felt like the wagon train was another town that she was visiting instead of a home.

Despite being a nomadic tribe, when the wagon train settled down friends, families, and fellow workers would pitch close to each other, creating impromptu streets, squares, and encampments that down the years had been named. Sven and Sigrun strode down Lubben Street, and entered Hoedemaker Square.

This square was made up of small boxy wagons, which had weavers inside working on looms. Dominating the north end was a long and wide wagon that looked like a house. Standing at the front door, in a fine woven tunic and resting on his cane, was the figure of Yael Hoademaker. His chubby face gazed over the square with a look of control and satisfaction.

He nodded his head when Sven and Sigrun approached him. Sven nodded back, while Sigrun gave him a small bow. It felt like the right kind of gesture to do for an Elder, though she felt somewhat silly when both Sven and Yael burst out laughing.

"You'll have to tell her that the Jarl is higher than us," Yael said, raising his cane at Sven.

"Well today is going to be a day full of learning, if the weather holds up," Sven replied.

Sigrun felt like she was being talked down to, so straightened up and said, "Maybe you can tell me how it works then. What is the relationship between Elders like you and the Jarl, why do I get to make the decisions but you choose whether I get the role in the first place?"

"Have you not read your mother's books, a lot of the why is in there," Yael said, giving her a questioning look.

It was true that her mother had made a series of volumes that detailed the history of the wagon train, from its founding by the Mission of Sol to when her mother had been alive, but she had never found the recitation of events all that compelling or necessary to know. She loved the books because they were the last connection that she had to her mother, but she was more interested in hearing her retelling of the fables.

"Well, since you're not that interested in history I'll keep it brief," Yael said, clearing his throat. "For some time the Baldur's and the Hoademakers - this was decades before the Mattsons were invited in - wanted more control within the wagon train. They were sick and tired of the Mission of Sol controlling the laws and the destinations they went to. A general strike by both families brought our precious demands to us, but the faith had a clever trick up their sleeve. They stipulated that in an emergency the head of the wagon train could make decisions that changed laws or moved the train. And being in an icy world, with raiders and violent towns within, there were a lot of emergencies, and since the Elders at the time couldn't both be heads we didn't get a say in anything. So the Baldurs and the Hoademakers made a deal together, they would elect a head that would make decisions for the people. Thus the Jarl was born. There is obviously a lot more to the story, the families having to wrangle more so the Jarl's power could be legitimized, and a few stand offs when either side was pissed about the other's decisions, but that is probably more detail than you want."

Sigrun nodded. "Thank you for letting me know. So the Jarl is both powerful and beholden to you."

"Not me specifically, but the three of us. All three family Elders try to pick who is going to be Jarl"

"But there weren't three of you there last night, only two. And it looked to me like the Mattsons were not very happy about the whole reason for the feast."

Yael grimaced, and glanced at Sven. "This one is sharp, I give her that."

"We can make a politician out of her yet," Sven said, smiling. He turned to her. "You are right, Rita Mattson was not one of the people at the party to vote for the new Jarl, neither did she vote out the previous one. The only reason Hannes is not Jarl anymore is because of a vote in the Council."

"Why did you vote Hannes out?" she asked.

Yael rubbed the silver spinning wheel. "I feel it might be best if me and Gregor tell you that together. It is something you will have to be aware of as the new leader. But you should settle into your new wagon first."

"New wagon?" she said, surprised.

"You don't think you're going to be Jarl in your beaten up, splinter filled wagon do you?" Sven said, chuckling. "You are going up in the world so the place you stay needs to suit."

"Oh, that reminds me," Sigrun said, feeling that now was as good a time as any to request this. "I think I'm going to need a new wardrobe. None of my clothes fit my new station."

Yael nodded. "I'll get on it right away."

The Jarl's home struck Sigrun as the most opulent wagon in the whole wagon train. While many painted bright colours on their homes, the Jarl's wagon had an explosion of colors swirling across its mahogany. The dominant color was a bright red, the same color as Manang in the sky, while on top were patterns of gold creating what looked like a forest of trees. In between these patterns were various different runes, some of them of the Baldur, Hoademaker, and Mattson family. The wagon's square frame stood on top of gleaming silver bars and four yellow painted wheels.

Sigrun was surprised to get to go into the wagon let alone live in it. This wagon felt like one that she would be steered away from, and she would only be allowed in if she did something spectacular or something very bad. She glanced towards Sven to make sure this really wasn't an elaborate joke, but his amused look didn't give anything away. He gestured towards the door, which had a silver doorknob and frosted window pane.

Surprisingly, the inside was more cozy than opulent. The mahogany gave the space a dim light, great for meetings where friends drank whiskey. On the right wall was a large wardrobe, and on the left a small fireplace with a floral decorated coal box which could contain a crackling fire. The far back had a four poster bed with a silver curtain hung from wooden bars. Dominating the room was a wide desk with a felt green top, and arrayed around were comfy looking armchairs.

Stacked neatly on top of the desk were various scrolls and pieces of paper. Sigrun peaked at a few. The scrolls were large maps of the local area, and the papers were various different laws that could be brought in, and the people on the Council that would most likely vote for them. One thing that caught her eye was a note about settling down. One of the lines talked about the problems of the Mission of Sol and how the only way they'd get permission to settle down was to get rid of them entirely. Seeing that made Sigrun feel a little uncomfortable, what had Hannes been planning?

Sven stood at the door, examining the room like he belonged in it. "So what do you think of your new place?"

She felt a sense that she didn't belong here. Even if she scrubbed up clean, sorted out the mess of hair, and wore fancy tunics, she still only had experience of herding cows and drinking at parties. What did she know about what laws to bring in, what experience did she have of the world that would tell her where the wagon train should go, what relationships did she have that she could use to convince people to go with what she wanted?

"Are you sure you've made the right decision here?"

Sven stepped closer. His smile disappeared. "There were many that night we could have chosen, many with more experience of how to lead people, or had more connections with the families. But what Yael told my father, which convinced him, is that they were all too bland and safe. Most of them just talked about who we would trade with next, what potential resources we could take from the land, or how to keep our power against the Mission. Some of them just told us what we wanted to hear or worse just said they would do whatever we asked. None of them said what you said, how we were going about it all wrong, how we could have a vision of the future. All of them were tweaking around the edges, trying to keep what we already have, you gave us a chance to reach for greater than that."

"Yeah, but it's one thing to have that vision and another to fulfill it. Am I really the best person to do that?"

"Yes because you see it clearly and so you'll know how to bring it about. We will help you with the rest, you're not alone," Sven said, putting a hand on her shoulder.

Sigrun examined him. There was a lot more depth to Sven than a lot of people realized. On the surface he seemed to not take anything seriously, but it turned out that he had thought about things to a good degree and knew what to say. It comforted her. Someone like that could be a good ally for her to have, though they could also be a worse enemy - you would never know if they were really on your side until it was too late.

"So how's it going to work, me living here?" she asked, feeling a bit more sure of herself. She had gone for this job after all. "What's going to happen to my wagon and my cows?"

"I'm sure we can find some lone farmer to take up cattle ranching. You'd be surprised how many say they want to do it, thinking that it's an easy and quiet job."

"Well tell them that it's anything but easy. You have to wake up early in the morning, convince a herd of cows to come out of their pen, keep an eye on them so they don't do anything stupid like run out of the Sol Shard's protection and freeze to death, and not to mention you have to clean the shit out of the trailer every day. The quiet part is correct, but that eventually gets to you after a while and you get the desire to talk to anyone no matter what it's about."

"I'll make sure not to say any of that, I want people to actually go for the job," Sven said, laughing.

Sigrun smiled. She looked around the room still not believing that this was actually happening. She was going to be Jarl.

Then it dawned on her how big a move that was going to be. All her life had been in her cattle rancher's wagon, all her parents' life, and their parents. It was a big shift, and she worried for a second whether her parents would have approved. Maybe her father might not have, but her mother certainly would. Her mother had pursued her writing even though she had to look after Sigrun, and she always told Sigrun that she could do anything if she put her mind to it. Hearing those words again brought warmth in Sigrun's heart and made her fear about the move dissipate.

"How am I going to move my stuff?" she asked.

"Ah, I have something for that. Let me quickly run to Bonde Square and I'll get it for you."

Sven rushed out of the wagon, leaving Sigrun alone. While waiting, she wandered around the room, feeling the smooth wood planks, opening the wardrobe and pretending fantastic clothes were hung up, lying on the bed, and testing the armchair.

She sat behind the desk and pretended some important family member was in front of her. What would her attitude towards them be? Would she be the demanding things done type, or the be your friend type? She felt her natural inclination was the latter, but sometimes that could backfire. If you were friends with everyone, people might think you were weak and they could take advantage of it. Sometimes it might go the other way and people stopped trusting you, feeling your friendliness was fake. But she understood that being a hard nut wasn't any better, making people feel hostile towards you wasn't usually a good way to get people to accept your will.

There were so many avenues and potential pitfalls to think about. How would she get both the people and the important leaders on her side?

How would she solve the problem Hannes clearly had with the Mission of Sol. It hurt her brain thinking about it all, which made her question again what she was doing in the Jarl role. But she told herself that she was going to try it at least, she couldn't second guess everything before she did it. If she did she wouldn't get anything done, nor would the vision Sven talked about be fulfilled.

Sven came back with a wheelbarrow. Seeing it couldn't help but make Sigrun laugh. "All my stuff is going to go in there?"

"You might have to do several trips, sorry it's the best I can do," Sven said, chuckling.

Sigrun shook her head. "If that's the best you can do for a Jarl I might have to find someone else."

She stood up and took the handles of the wheelbarrow. She guessed she had to get back to gather all her things. Not to mention her cows did need some fresh air and lovely grass, even if it was raining.

Sven must have seen some hesitation in her, because he said, "You know we do have other people we can choose to be Jarl."

"Is that for if I don't want the job, or for when

I screw up too much?"

Sven laughed, and nodded his head. "You'll do fine, especially if you keep that humor."

She grinned, trying to appear confident and sure. "I'll do better than fine, I'll be the best damn Jarl you've ever seen."

FOR SOL TO COME BACK THE WORLD NEEDS TO BE FREE FROM SHADOW

'Scroll of Mission'

Rain pelted down on Sonja. Her hair felt slimy and her face went numb. Droplets went down her back, making her shiver. Wagons had already driven over the grass several times, so the water hitting the ground just created a swirl of mud. On several occasions she found her boot getting stuck into it, and she had to pull on her leg to keep walking.

She looked back through the streets and wondered whether she should stop this stupidity and go back to the encampment. But she remembered all the faithful staring at her, those piercing eyes of expectation, shuddered again, and kept on walking.

However, the stare that haunted her the most in her mind, and made her the most afraid about being the Keeper, was the one on her mother's portrait. Those wise eyes and passionate face seemed to tell her that she could be Keeper.

She couldn't be Keeper, she knew that with certainty. She was too full of shadow, too full of the burning desire for women, and too sick of hiding it any longer. If the faithful knew the truth about her they would strip the title of Keeper in a heartbeat, and tell her to get out of the enclosure.

So was that what she was doing now? Was she finally running away from the faith for good? She wasn't too sure.

One of the things that haunted her about the stares the faithful gave when she was named Keeper were their certainty. They expected her to be Keeper, expected her to fulfill the role, and even though some cursed her for that they automatically gave her a look of respect because of it. And that look of respect was an intoxicating thing.

In her adulthood, Sonja had always felt empty and felt the Mission might not be for her any more, but the one thing that kept her going was the respect and authority she got from being a senior Priestess. She was a General, which meant organizing the patrols across the wagon train, looking out for trouble in the distance, and defending the wagon train from raiders.

That last one had happened twice in her role as General. She could still remember the smell of fear from the faithful around, and the roar of the raiders as they rushed at her. Before and during the battle she had felt sick in her stomach, but when they won, she had felt an elation so joyful that she had thought for one split second she could give up sex for it.

The looks of respect and praise she got for doing her job were sometimes worth going through the pain of not being able to be who she was. Whenever she would think about quitting the faith, she would wonder what kind of job she would have in the wider wagon train. Would she be a farmer, a weaver, a cattle rancher? All those jobs felt empty in comparison to the one she was doing now, they didn't feel like she would be able to pursue something bigger than herself. Because that's what she felt being a General in the Mission. She felt that she was doing it for a bigger cause, that her actions would bring back Sol in the sky and bring paradise back into the world.

She ran to the edge of the caravan, where the hill dropped down to the valley below. She looked at the thick blanket of snow across the plain, the frozen ice floating in the river, the needles of white that formed the canopy of the forest. They couldn't compare to the lush green grass, the deep blue water, and the golden autumn of the world that she was taught in the scrolls. How could anyone accept living in this icy and cold landscape?

But she also couldn't accept living the way she was now. There were dark times in the past where she thought the easiest thing to do was to walk out of the protective bubble of the Sol Shard and freeze to death. She wouldn't have to feel the feeling of horrible desire, the wrench of shame, nor would her true self be discovered by her friends so she wouldn't disappoint them. No, she could just be someone they found in the middle of the snow, a tragic end to someone that symbolized so much good within the Mission.

She looked down the hill. Could that be the answer?

No. Ever since seeing the lifeless bodies of the children in the workhouse she grew up in, she understood that death was never as clean as she imagined it to be. It was always a horrible trauma for everyone that witnessed it. She wanted to live. But she also knew she couldn't be the Keeper. Could she?

Sonja looked out at Kveg Plain, at the shabby wagons dotted about the grass. Could she really live this life? One Cattle Rancher stood several yards away, she had blond hair with a braid trailing at the back, and her tunic and trousers seemed to be covered in mud. She was putting a hand up to the herd of cows next to her, and stomping to and fro sideways. It seemed fascinating to Sonja, the movement looked almost like dancing. Could she really learn how to do that, would it be as satisfying as being the head of a religion?

But would being the head of a religion be all that satisfying for her, a religion that didn't allow her to be who she wanted to be, a religion whose teachings said that loving the gender she did was wrong for the world. And if she was head of that religion those would be the things she would have to teach. She would have to project an image of purity, when really she was just as muddy as the cattle rancher.

Everyone else in the faith seemed to be clean. She sometimes wondered whether it was a true reflection, whether some of them were harboring shadows like hers. But she couldn't ask because they would reject it, feeling you were attacking their commitment in the faith. Surely she couldn't be the only person with shadow, but even if she wasn't it still felt like she was. And that made her alone.

She sighed, it was all too confusing and complicated. There was no decision she could make that made her feel happy. Being the Keeper would make her feel empty inside, and being a regular person in the wagon train would make her feel without purpose. It was a horrible decision, and she cursed the world for having to make it. Why couldn't Sol make it easy?

Sonja shook her head, and went to walk back to the encampment. She still had no idea what she would do about those stares.

Sonja trudged across Kveg Plain. Unfortunately, the ground had become even more waterlogged and muddy, meaning that with every third step her boot would get stuck. The sky above was covered by a black cloud, which crackled with electricity. Not wanting to be struck by lightning, Sonja strode faster.

Her foot squelched into the ground. It had gone below the swirl of brown mud. She tried to pull herself out but her foot wouldn't budge. She kept twisting and pulling but the ground would not let her go. She grunted in frustration, realizing she would have to get someone to help her. She turned back to the blond cattle rancher that stood in the distance. The cattle rancher had her back to Sonja, but she was clearly trying to keep control of her cows. Sonja could hear their distressed moos.

She was about to shout to the rancher, when a flash of lightning struck behind the cows. Smoke rose quickly above the herd. The cows all cried in alarm, and hoofed away from the flames behind. The cattle rancher had to jump out of their way.

The cows were now stampeding towards Sonja.

She tried to twist her boot frantically. She bent down and grabbed at her ankles, pulling with all her effort, not caring if she left the boot behind. The thunder of the hooves mixed with the crack of thunder in the sky. Sonja's heart thumped louder and louder. She screamed, and savagely scratched and punched her boot and leg in a desperate attempt

to get them to release.

She looked up, the cows were nearly on her. She would not make it in time.

A tear fell down her cheek. She didn't want to die. She had never truly loved another person, never been in a long term relationship with anyone, had never felt that surge of joy that she heard her friends talk about feeling with their husbands. All the relations she had with other women had just been for sex, and usually of a transactional nature. It had always been fun at the time, but it never grew beyond that. And afterwards she always felt that shame and sense of emptiness. She wanted to feel more, but she was never going to.

Mud flew in the air. She could smell the cows stink as they got closer. She closed her eyes, trying not to think about how stupid an end this was. Other Keepers had been killed by raiders, or executed by rulers, or nicely in their sleep. But she would be killed by stampeding cows. Maybe it would have been better just to freeze after all.

She scrunched up her face, only feeling the vibration of the ground. A great force hit her, knocking all her breath out.

The thing that Sonja found weird about death was how it didn't feel that much different to life. She was sure the cows must have hit her, and her soul was now in the place where Sol resided. But she still felt the squishy mud on her back and the drips of rain on her skin. The only thing that felt different was that a great weight pressed on her front.

Wanting to know what Sol's resting place was like, and what could be weighing on her, Sonja opened her eyes. All she could see was a sky full of black clouds. The rain pattered down on her face, and she could hear the faint sound of cows mooing in the distance.

She was alive.

That information shocked her. She was sure that the cows had been too close to get out of the way. She laughed, feeling a joy so big that she couldn't help but want to jump up and dance about. But there was still that weight on top of her.

She looked down to see what it was. It was a person, a woman in fact. It was the blond haired cattle rancher that had been trying to control the cows. The woman's arms were thick, like the arms of the Priestesses that she liked to stare at. Her face had a strong jawline and fierce eyes. In fact Sonja couldn't help admit that she found her saviour quite attractive.

The cattle rancher pushed herself off, and offered a hand. Sonja took it.

She felt a tingle go up her hand and through her body. A rush of warmth went up to her head. She felt dizzy.

And then Sonja found herself leaning over and kissing the woman.

The action was a shock to her, as it was to the blond haired woman. The woman with the braid widened her eyes and pushed her away. Sonja felt totally embarrassed, having no idea what she was doing. She glanced towards the woman, a little embarrassed. They seemed to stand there close to one another awkwardly. Sonja stepped back. The woman with the braid put her hand in her hair and laughed.

"Well I'm glad you're ok. Usually people know my name before that happens. It's Sigrun by the way."

"Sonja," she said. Her face felt hot. "Sorry about the kiss, the situation and the push to the ground must have made me lose my senses."

"I don't mind getting a kiss as a reward for my heroics, especially by a beautiful girl like you," Sigrun said, staring at her with the kind of stare Sonja must have had when she stared at women she liked.

Did Sigrun find other women attractive? Sonja knew that some women in the wider wagon train were like that, she did sleep with some of them at parties, but she had never known how wide spread the feelings of same sex love were and always felt ashamed to find out in case it got back to the faith.

"You must have lost your senses as well if you find me attractive," she said, brushing her black hair away, which she now felt was full of mud. She would definitely need a bath, another reason why Sigrun's assessment of her must not be true.

Sigrun stepped closer and smudged her finger across Sonja's cheek. "You're a bit muddy, but I'd definitely want a drink with you."

Sonja's heart pounded like mad. The touch of Sigrun's was only a few seconds but she definitely wanted more. They stood, staring at each other. Sigrun's eyes were bright blue, burning with clear desire.

"In fact," Sigrun said, smiling. "Let me return the favor."

Sigrun leant forward and kissed her. It was like Sonja's body got struck by lightning. She could feel every part of her body buzzing. Her head felt light. A burning desire ran through her, she wanted to grab a hold of Sigrun's tunic and push her down in the mud.

But she stopped herself. Sonja had told herself that she didn't just want sex she wanted a relationship: someone that wanted to know her, talk to her, and care about her. Having sex with this woman now would not lead to that. She stepped back

Sigrun also stepped back. She looked awkward and embarrassed. "Sorry, I should have asked whether you wanted that. Now I'm the one whose senses have been lost."

Sonja didn't want this woman to think that she had done something wrong. She wanted to be able to see her again. "I liked it, I just think we should have a drink first."

"That sounds good," Sigrun said, a little breathless. "All my drink is in the wagon over there, maybe come over one evening. Though tomorrow I'm not going to be at that wagon, I'm going to be at the Jarl's wagon."

Sonja's eyes widened in surprise. She had just kissed the future leader of the wagon train!

Sigrun laughed. "Don't worry it came as a shock to me as well." She glanced behind Sonja, grimacing. "Sorry about this, but I'm going to have to sort out those cows. I don't want them hurting anyone else. I can't be asking multiple women back to my wagon today."

She patted Sonja's shoulders, gave her another

grin, and ran off into the muddy field. Sonja turned and watched her race towards the cows, who weren't stampeding anymore but they were roaming quickly across the grass.

Sonja still felt light headed and a little woozy, but she couldn't feel the patter of rain on her hair anymore. The clouds in the sky broke apart. A small ray of red shone down. It felt like all of her worries and questions about being a Keeper had fallen away. Now, her brain buzzed, and it did it for one person: Sigrun.

ALWAYS CONNECT BACK TO YOUR PAST, IT'LL BE YOUR LIGHT IN THE DARKNESS, THE THING THAT CAN SHOW YOU THE PATH AHEAD

'Meditations' by Wilbur Paige

Sigrun laughed at the craziness of yesterday. She had saved a woman from stampeding cows and had gotten two kisses out of it. Afterwards she had wondered whether it had been a weird dream, only the mud on her trousers and tunic indicated it hadn't been. She kind of wished that she could see Sonja again, have that drink together, but she didn't know when she would turn up again, if she ever would. And at the moment she had some moving to do.

The inside of her home was shabby and messy: the wooden slats that made up the wagon were faded and peeling away, the rug on the floor had several hairs tufted out, the wardrobe door looked like it was about to fall off at any moment, the desk in the corner had so much dust over it, and the shelf on the left wall was slightly askew. But it was still her home, and it felt wrong to be packing it up like this. She didn't even know whether all her stuff would fit in the wheelbarrow Sven had given her. She just would have to find out.

She started with the shelf, which held her mother's books. They all had yellow-brown jackets with gold lettering on the spine. Most of it was filled up with volumes of *'The History of the Wagon Train'*. Her mother had gone out and spoken to the older people of the caravan to see if they knew any stories about how it had been founded. This meant going to the Keeper and some of the older Priests and Priestesses, because the Mission was the one that had ultimately founded the wagon train. Her mother pursued the whole endeavor with passion and exuberance, trying to write down every family the wagon train added, every fight the different people within had, and every major milestone that came about. It was a towering achievement for her mother, and the thing that had made her famous within the train. But they weren't Sigrun's favorite.

Sigrun's favorite book was the thick book right at the end of the shelf. The gold lettering read *'How Manang Ate The Sun, And Other Fables'*. As a child, tucked up in bed with the covers up to Sigrun's nose, her mother would read from this book. But it wasn't just any reading. Her mother would narrate it with a dramatic voice, whenever the characters would speak she would give them a funny little accent, and when they would do some actions her mother would act them out herself.

Sigrun held the book reverentially. She smelt it, and even though it smelled like old dust it couldn't help but transform into the smell of her mother, like sweet peaches. She felt a dull ache in her heart, and a tear ran down her cheek.

It still surprised her how much the pain of her mother's death still affected her. She had been told time healed your wounds, which she found to be both true and untrue. Sure, the pain she felt about her mother wasn't as raw as the day she died - that had felt deep and scarring, like a black void that had swallowed her up - but neither was the pain fully gone. It was still deep down inside, and sometimes she would wake up feeling it like a weight. Those days would be the hardest to get through.

She carefully placed *'How Manang Ate The Sun'* and the volumes of *'The History of the Wagon Train'* in the wheelbarrow. The next place she went to for personal items were the drawers underneath the bed. In here she took out a square wooden box, which had an engraved title on the front: *'The King's Game'*.

The boardgame was the only present she got from her father. They had played *'The Kings Game'* together for many years. When her father played he didn't treat her like a child. He would play advanced tactics and moves, and when he resoundly beat her he would gloat. This would infuriate Sigrun, driving her to find any tactic in order for her to win. She would think about the games they had played, and experimented with different moves or strategies. Every time she got beaten again she would experiment some more. Eventually the work paid off.

One glorious afternoon, when Manang was high in the sky and the smell of flowers were within the air, Sigrun and her father had their final match. It was tense, and lasted several hours, but in the end she beat him, capturing his king. It was her time to gloat. He laughed and told her he was impressed. As a present for winning he said she could keep the game.

She placed *'The Kings Game'* into the wheelbarrow. The next thing she took out of her drawer was a sword. After her parents died she was angry at the world, so she bought a sword. At night she would sneak within the Mission's encampment to practice. At the time she didn't know who she was going to fight. Her father, a big target of her anger because he had drifted away as soon as her mother had gotten sick, had already walked outside the wagon train and had frozen to death. Still, she felt like she wanted to attack or kill someone for taking away her mother. Thankfully, the process of trying to get better at sword fighting instilled a discipline within. This made the anger slowly dissipate. Unfortunately for her it was replaced by an empty feeling.

The final items from the drawer were two whiskey bottles. These, and the parties she attended, were the ways she had masked her empty feelings. Getting drunk, talking to people, and fucking, had been very good at getting rid of the numbness inside. How could you feel your life was going nowhere when you were blind drunk most of the time? Well after a few years she did actually start feeling it, but she couldn't think of anything else to do so kept on partying.

Now with the Jarl job she had a chance to change her life, and this new responsibility automatically gave her a purpose.

She opened up the wardrobe, but decided to not take any of the clothes. None of them screamed Jarl material to her.

She turned back to the wheelbarrow. Books, a

board game, a sword, and two whiskey bottles, that was the extent of her life. Seeing it all laid bare made her feel small. She imagined that many of the others at the feast that had wanted to be Jarl would have tonnes of treasures that would have needed several wheelbarrows. There's would probably be filled with pendants, necklaces, swords, shields, furniture, and fine drinking glasses. Maybe when she was Jarl she would buy some for herself.

She looked around the wagon one last time, wiping the desk of dust, straightening the rug, and doing her bed. It now felt strangely empty, like the items she had taken out had also taken out the wagon's soul. Sigrun was never going to see this place again, so she put her hand on the wood and said goodbye. She grabbed hold of the wheelbarrow handles, and pushed it out of the door.

IN REALITY THE SCROLLS ARE WRITTEN IN STORIES, TEACHINGS, AND MYTH. EVERY KEEPER HAS TO INTERPRET IT IN THEIR OWN WAY, AND TEACH THEIR INTERPRETATIONS TO THE MASSES

'Diary of the Heretic Keeper' by Unknown

Sonja stumbled through the Mission of Sol's encampment in a daze. Her thoughts were on Sigrun: her blond hair and braid, her fierce face, her thick arms, and the two kisses. Her breath still caught a little thinking on them.

The light headedness and the feeling of euphoria slowly dimmed as she walked past the dormitory wagons and the training yard. Seeing Priests and Priestess in their yellow robes brought her back to the reality of the faith. The faithful would have called what she did with Sigrun a grave shadow. They would feel she was going against Sol with her wretched thoughts, and they would exile her. She could not have what she wanted in this encampment.

By the time she got to the yellow wood pews her thoughts had become bitter. What was so wrong with the feelings that she felt for Sigrun, how were they any less to the ones Priestesses had for farmers? Why did the fact that she was feeling it for someone of the same gender automatically make it come from Manang? It didn't make sense in her eyes, but it had been so ingrained into the Acolytes from an early age that many would feel it made total sense.

It made her feel empty and dissatisfied. She could never be in the faith, they would never accept her.

Sonja walked up to the Keeper's wagon, and found her friends waiting for her. Roose, Britta, and Teresa all had looks of concern, and rushed up to see how she was doing. Roose examined her robes, which were so caked full of mud that you could hardly see their yellow.

"What happened to you, Keeper?" Roose said.

Sonja gave her a strange glance, Keeper? And then she remembered why she ran away.

"We were worried about you," Britta said, squeezing her arm. "We had feared your running away might have meant you didn't want to be Keeper."

Did she want to be Keeper? When it had been announced she felt she couldn't be: she couldn't compare to her mother's leadership and she was too full of shadow. Nothing much had changed since she had run away really, but in a lot of ways it had. She had nearly died, she had met another woman, they had kissed, and it had all brought into her so clearly what she wanted.

Because all her thoughts while at the edge of the wagon train had been about how the faith gave her a sense of purpose, and she didn't feel the jobs in the wider train would give her that. But the near death experience and the meeting with Sigrun had unlocked the desire to love who she wanted and to not be ashamed of that. She wanted to be both in the faith and to love women.

"It was all so much. I felt I had to think about it a lot," she said to her friends.

"We understand," Teresa said, giving her a caring smile. "It's been an emotional time."

"Have you thought about your decision then, are you going to be Keeper?" Britta asked, biting her lip.

Sonja looked at them all, beautiful Britta with the golden curls, thin and tall Roose with the smoky eyes, and short and dumpy Teresa with the kind smile. Would they really want her to be Keeper if she told them the truth, would the Mission? She didn't totally think so, but would there be a way to change that? It felt that same sex love being wrong was a matter of being taught it, and if they were taught to hate it then surely they might be able to be taught to accept it? If she could teach them that someone that loved the same gender could still praise Sol and still be good, then they might just be able to change their attitude. And then she might be accepted for once. And there was only one way to change the teachings of the Mission.

"I have decided to accept the Keeper position," she said.

Roose and Teresa exclaimed in joy, and hugged her. However Britta had a look of disappointment. It went away as soon as Sonja saw it, but she understood that Britta still felt that the Keeper job should have gone to her. Sonja wondered how she was going to deal with that.

"I won't deny I've been worried whether another Keeper would come in and take away my job," Britta said, giving her a fake smile.

Roose hit her in the arm. "It's not about you."

"It's fine, I understand. But the exciting thing is that we can still work together. Though it also means you are going to have to follow my orders, whatever I say."

"Tch, I can't believe I'm going to be bossed by a youngster," Teresa said, grinning.

"I'm sure the pupils would love to see the new Keeper," Britta said, glancing behind her.

Sonja saw many Priests, Priestesses, and Acolytes hanging nearby. They looked like they were performing their jobs, but clearly they were listening in on the group's conversation. "I'm sure the whole Mission would like to as well. Probably the whole wagon train, just to see who they need to hate now."

Britta frowned. "They're all bunch of stupid shadow filled people. I don't get why we tolerate them not being faithful to our commandments. This is our wagon train."

She put a hand on her shoulder. "They are not all bad, they will see the light if we show it to them."

Britta didn't say anything but she didn't look convinced.

"So are you going to be making a speech?" Teresa asked.

"I think before I do a lot of learning about the role is in order. I think I will read the scrolls, just to see if I can glean anything from them."

"I would have thought you would have all the

scrolls memorized by now," Roose said.

"Well I have memorized the important ones, but none that I can remember say what the Keeper's duties actually are. Besides, I want to look into something." She clasped their shoulders and gave them all another hug. "You get on with your jobs, you don't want to be hanging around me while I read."

The inside of the Keeper's wagon was still as dark as it had been that morning, when Sonja had stood in front of her mother's coffin. The coffin wasn't there anymore, and the painting had been moved to the glass cabinet on the right wall.

The cabinet contained urns, necklaces, and boxes from the significant Priestesses, Priests, and Keepers from the Mission's history. The top half had rows of paintings of all the previous Keepers, most of them looked as leaderly and wise as her mother. Sonja wondered whether her painting would look just as regal and benevolent, and realized it was kind of crazy that she was going to get a painting, that she actually decided to be Keeper.

The only light that could be seen in the wagon came from the Sol Shard, a deep orange glow. She stared at the shard, wanting to touch it. This was hers to keep and protect. She wondered if she touched it whether she would feel Sol herself.

She shook her head, she had too much to do to stand and stare at the Sol Shard. Since she was the new Keeper it was her job to make sure this area was brightly lit, the rule of the Keeper's wagon was that no shadow was allowed to be cast. She took out a match from a drawer and lit every torch and candle within. Every torch banished a large area of gloom, while each candle cast out the little shadows in the gaps between. Soon it was so bright it hurt Sonja's eyes to look at any one part of the wagon.

Once she was done, she went to the glass cabinet that stood on the left. In here, placed neatly on glass shelves, were many scrolls rolled up in mahogany wood. These were the sacred scrolls, the foundation of the Mission of Sol. They had been written by Keeper Joan, who had wanted all the faith's teachings, stories, and history recorded. This was to make sure the tenants and commandments of their faith could be solidified and made permanent.

However, only the Keeper and the Head Teacher were allowed to see the scrolls. This meant that the solidified grounding sometimes shifted depending on the Keeper. Her mother's teaching had been obsessed with purity. She banned drinking alcohol, and eating meat - though some rumors said this was more because the Mattsons refused to give them any meat - and drilled into every acolyte the importance of keeping any kind of shadow out of your lives. It was these teachings which had made Sonja feel miserable, and why she grew distanced from her mother near the end.

She opened up the glass case, and scanned the gold lettering on the wood. She wanted to read the scrolls that would tell her why being gay was a shadow. If she could see the faithful's reasoning she might have more of an idea of what she could do to change people's minds. And if the scrolls said categorically that it was a shadow and no one should change their mind, then she finally had her answer on whether to stay in the faith. But she doubted it would be that concrete.

The scrolls' wisdom usually came from speeches of important faithful, or from stories. A lot of time in class Sonja wouldn't always understand what these stories or speeches were trying to say, until a teacher would tell them how it related to this action or that shadow. Sometimes she questioned whether these passages really meant what the teacher said, but since she couldn't read the scrolls at the time she had to take their word for it. Now she could actually check them.

She slid out the Scroll of Shadow, thinking this would probably have the mention of same sex love. She took it over to the desk, underneath the Sol Shard, and rolled it out. She sat down, and skimmed through to find a passage she was looking for. She found it near the beginning of the scroll.

> Aileas and his clan stood shocked as the last remnants of Sol turned to dust within the sky. The tribe saw the glittering of crystals raining down onto the earth, and felt the shiver of cold. Aileas knew that humanity was on its last days and it was up to them to survive. He called on his clan to go towards the crystals.
>
> On the trip, Aileas went through his clan to see if they were hardy enough to survive the new world. He was thankful to see many strong armed men and women amongst his clan, but one sight disturbed him greatly. A man sitting by the fire, holding hands with another man.
>
> Aileas' voice boomed. "How can you be with a man when you have just seen the destruction of the

world?" The two men were confused and asked what was wrong with being with a man. Aileas replied, "We are the last of our kind, and if we don't want our song to be the last heard we must produce children and make sure they are hardy. A man cannot have children with another man."

The men protested, but the others in the clan saw the wisdom in Aileas' words. Their clan would need offspring if their race was to survive. Thus they brought in laws banning the act of same sex love, and demanded the two men separate and take wives.

Sonja reread it again, a little confused. But after another reading she understood that was it. The reason why being gay was considered a shadow was because it didn't produce babies. Maybe back in the chaos of Sol's demise she could see the pragmatism of wanting babies, especially for Aileas clan who thought they were the only ones left, but it had been many centuries since that was the case. The wagon train passed through many settlements, towns, and cities full of humans. Humanity seemed to have weathered the storm and was coming back into prominence. Besides, there were a few Priests and Priestess in the celibacy movement, who believed purity was in not having any relationships or sex. A lot of the mainstream faithful believed this to be strange, but they didn't feel it was a shadow. So if that was the case, why was being gay considered one?

Sonja sat back, shaking her head. Would the other shadows be the same way, would they have just as tenuous an explanation? She went back to the glass cabinet and took out a few more scrolls, ones she knew would have teachings about over drinking and overeating. The one that she focused on most was Priest Robin's account, as that focused on the supposed connection with partying and corruption.

The account wasn't any better. Most of the connections Robin made were based on feelings rather than fact. Robin thought the city he was in was more corrupt because of the parties but Sonja thought it could be the other way around: the city was more corrupt so they had more decadent parties.

It made Sonja go through every single scroll to see if they were the same. She spent many days in the Keeper's wagon, pouring over teachings and stories to figure out if anything her mother did was actually based on any real evidence. By the end she found none.

INFORMATION IS CRUCIAL TO HAVE AS A KING, THAT'S WHY MANY TRY TO HOARD IT, OR ONLY GIVE IT TO YOU FOR A PRICE

'The Unhappy King' by Lysanne Lungbourg

Gregor and Yael sat opposite Sigrun. Yael had a dark green coat over his fine tunic, and his chubby face looked over at Sigrun appreciatively. Gregor looked tired and his face pale, his hands shook when they rubbed his braided beard. It definitely seemed that Gregor was sick with something, but Sigrun had been too polite to ask what it was.

The two Elders explained to her the political situation she found herself in as Jarl. In the past when some guy – and it was always a guy – talked about the politics of the wagon train she would space out and think about the cute redhead that was dancing around the bonfire, but she understood that now she had to pay attention.

"After harvest the Keeper usually picks the destination," Gregor said, his meaty hands unfurling a map on the desk. "Since we got a new Keeper I'm not too sure where she will take us, but if we see on the map there are two options." He followed the river, the Is, with his finger. "The Town of Munn, and," he then placed his finger in the middle of the Glass Forest, "The City of Eik."

Sigrun noticed that next to the City of Eik was a large cross. "Why is that there?"

"The Queen of Eik really doesn't like the Mission," Yael said, leaning on his cane. "About a decade ago some proselytizers gained some traction with the revolutionaries and outsiders. As you can imagine they caused a lot of trouble for the Queen. When we went back there we were nearly taken prisoner, took a lot of wrangling to get us out of that mess. The Mission won't admit it, they'll feel it's a great city to visit, but if the Keeper chooses that city you'll want to say no. Make it a vote in the Council if you have to."

Sigrun nodded. The lecture they had given her before this discussion had been about the Council, how even though the Jarl could bring in laws themselves it was always best to get them voted in by the Council as they were more likely to stick. The council was composed of the five important people on the workers and faithful side.

"So I guess then the only option is the City of Munn," she said.

"Not necessarily," Gregor said. "We are about

to have a harvest which means we have plenty of supplies. The wagon train could easily take a month or two before going to the next town."

"You were there when it was announced Gregor, do we know who this new Keeper is and what path she is likely to pick?" she asked.

"It was one of the 'daughters' of the Keeper, Sonja I believe her name is."

The name Sonja struck her heart like lightning. Was it the same Sonja that she had saved and kissed? It couldn't be, not if she was in the faith. There was not many things she knew about the Mission but the one thing she definitely knew was that they hated people who were gay.

As a young child Sigrun attended prayers with her mother. At the time she didn't mind praying to Sol and hearing the sermons about being good, but that all changed when one of the sermons was about how being gay was a shadow and should be stamped out. After hearing that, knowing that it applied to her, she refused to attend prayers anymore.

"I feel I probably should meet this new Keeper," she said.

"It's probably a good idea, but be careful," Yael said. "You don't want to appear too friendly towards the Keeper. Many of my workers don't like their influence, and it's becoming clear that quite a few of Gregor's workers are feeling the same."

Gregor fingered his Sol necklace, grimacing. "Yes, our family has definitely not liked the purity agenda the last Keeper pursued. They basically outlawed a lot of things my workers liked. It made it difficult to keep allying with them. My own workers nearly revolted when they heard I had voted with them to cast out Hannes."

"Ah yes, Hannes, that's another thing I wanted to understand," Sigrun said. "Why did you vote him out?"

"He was stealing our food," Gregor shouted.

The outburst surprised her and Yael. Yael squeezed Gregor's arm to calm him down. "Yes, Hannes was using his connection with the Administrator to take food for his parties. And these weren't the usual every month feasts or celebrations, these were every week. Can you imagine a feast every week being held, the amount of food that would be used?"

Sigrun could imagine it because she had been to those parties. The tables had been heaving with meat, cheese, and vegetables. At the time she loved the fact that the parties were more frequent, and she definitely enjoyed herself to that food and drink, but now she understood what that meant to the wider wagon train. They were a nomadic tribe that sometimes didn't see civilization for a few months, wasting that much food and having none left could have led to starvation.

"Please tell me that Hannes was just taking extra stock."

Gregor shook his head. He stroked the braids in his beard vigorously. "No, he wasn't using extra stock. He was using the normal stores, and they got pretty empty. He tried to mask it by going to the town of Matt. He told us all it was just a trading mission, but since we had already been in another town recently we were very suspicious. That's when we found out about the stores. After that revelation we had to vote him out. He was lucky there was a town to get food from, if we were outside of civilization he would have starved us."

She understood Gregor's anger and sympathized with it, Hannes actions were reckless and stupid. The only troubling question she had was why, why did Hannes create frequent parties every week? She guessed Hannes wasn't totally stupid and would have understood using that much food wasn't going to be sustainable for a nomadic tribe. He must have had some endgame in mind. But what was it? Was it just to be popular amongst the people? That was good for a leader but she didn't feel it would be worth all that risk, if you wanted to be sure in your position as Jarl your best bet was to get the two people sitting in front of her on board. There was definitely something she was missing.

"Is there anything else I need to know about Hannes, why you voted against him?" she asked.

"Is that not enough?" exclaimed Gregor.

Yael held onto his arm again to calm him down. Sigrun noticed for a brief second a worried glance from Yael and Gregor in her direction, before they went back to their usual expressions. She might be reading into things, but the two of them were hiding something. And that something had to do with Hannes.

She put up her hands to Gregor. "I'm sorry I don't mean to dismiss the issues, it's just if I want to deal with this I need to know everything. So if there is something else you need to tell me about the situation it'd be good to know."

"There's nothing else to tell," Yael said, leaning back on his chair. "Except of course that the

Mattsons are punishing us because of our decision. I don't know why but Rita and her lot have tied their wagons to Hannes, and they are very pissed at him being thrown out. They are making sure we don't eat any meat at mealtimes!"

So Yael and Gregor were going to hide what they knew. What else did they want to hide from her, why were they hiding it? Had the two of them chosen her as Jarl not because they liked her vision, but to make a move against the Mattsons she was unaware of. She felt like a sacrificial piece within *'The King's Game'*.

She did her best to hide her disappointment and anxiety. She had to play this smartly, get the knowledge somehow and use it to her advantage in some way. God was this really the stuff she had to think about being the Jarl? Part of her wanted to go back to the simplicity of being a cattle rancher. She wouldn't have to think about political games then.

"And what's the food situation?" she asked Gregor, making sure to breathe normally. "Can we stop them from doing this stuff again?"

"Not totally, they still have the Administrator on their side who will give them whatever they want," Gregor said bitterly. "Damn I don't want our sweat and hard work in this harvest to go to waste to some stupid parties."

"Can you not just hoard the food for yourself?"

Yael shook his head. "The problem comes in the fact that the Mattsons cook for everybody. They control the communal mealtimes and what gets eaten. They make the bread. So if we don't give them ingredients they are going to make people starve for one or two mealtimes and definitely say why it happened."

"We already have grumbles from a lot of the farmers about Hannes. They understood the waste, but they still have a soft spot for him. If we appear too mean, Hannes will definitely use that energy against us."

"So this whole vote you did to stop him didn't do anything, we are still in the same position," she said, feeling the situation was hopeless.

Gregor put up his hands in frustration. "What were we supposed to do, turn a blind eye and let him continue starving us? Yes the situation hasn't changed but I still feel we did the right thing, just for the principle."

Sigrun nodded, leaning back on her chair, thinking. This was definitely a very tricky situation for her to deal with. What was she supposed to do? If she allowed Hannes to keep the food they would waste it again, if they stopped him from having it the Mattsons would punish the wagon train and tell everyone that it was Gregor's and Yael's fault. Both options seemed pretty bad to her. Was there a middle ground?

She turned to Yael. "Do you still have those ovens you bought from the merchants a few years back. I remember the rumors about it, how your family was able to cook their own food, not needing to do communal mealtimes."

"We do, but we only use it for fancy occasions and private get-togethers. It's only one so I don't feel we would be able to cook everyone's meal, plus we don't have the manpower. There is a reason the Mattsons became a very prominent family in a very short space of time, they understood the power in cooking everyone's food and seized it aggressively."

"What if we appear to be buying lots of the same ovens?" she said.

"What do you mean?" Yael asked.

"We go to Munn and we get the resources to make ovens and give them to the handymen. We then make a big play out of us giving them to everybody. The Mattsons will feel threatened and might be willing to come to the table and make a deal against Hannes to keep their power.

Yael sat there, rubbing his cane, thinking. Gregor seemed to be smiling. "I do like this idea.

Yael nodded. "Yeah, I like that idea. It could work."

"Good, I'll speak to this new Keeper and will try to convince her to go to Munn."

It would be good to see whether this Sonja was the same one that she had saved and kissed. She felt it couldn't be, but since she became Jarl she was prepared for any bizarre events to happen now.

Gregor and Yael nodded at her, and got up. Sigrun helped Yael to get out of his seat and across the floor. She examined him, his chubby face, and his neutral demeanor. She caught another slight worried glance from him. He was definitely not telling her something.

She would have to find out what was happening with Hannes, what was the true reason they had voted him out. And the best place she would get the answer would be from the people of the wagon train.

SOME PEOPLE LOVE CHANGE SO MUCH THEYLL ADORE YOU FOR IT, SOME HATE IT SO MUCH THEYLL KILL YOU TO STOP IT FROM HAPPENING

'Ilhan The Reformer' by Frey Hanne

Sonja sat back in her chair, staring down at the scrolls. All careful consideration for them had been thrown out of the window, they all were rolled out and piled up on top of each other. She had skimmed them all and came to the conclusion that the basis of purity within the Mission had been a lie. The rules and commandments of what was a good life had been cobbled together from various different stories and leaders throughout the history of the faith. When taken in the context of the times they were in, the rules and commandments made sense, but she didn't feel they made sense anymore. Those issues weren't as big in people's lives anymore.

But where did that leave the Mission? Part of its goal was to proselytize to others about leading a shadow free life and by doing so they would bring Sol back into the sky. If what was shadow was arbitrary and changed throughout time, what were they going to teach others? What were the teachings that the Mission could give to people?

Sonja felt a weight in her heart. Everything she felt she ever believed was crashing down inside her. The goal that she had dedicated her life to, that gave her life meaning, had been a false one. All those times that she felt she needed to be purer, the hate and shame she felt, had been hurtful wastes. Maybe she should just not be Keeper anymore, she clearly couldn't see the point of the Mission and why it taught what it did.

But she immediately rejected that feeling. There was something about the faith that kept her here, what was it?

She closed her eyes, she could feel the warmth of the Sol Shard at the back of her neck. It was a warm and cozy feeling, like being sat by a fireplace. She got up and turned around, opening her eyes. The orange glowed within the white crystal. It seemed to be pulsating, almost like it was speaking to her. She felt an urge to hold it.

She grabbed the crystal with both hands, feeling a burn. But there was no pain, instead the burn felt like a deep sense of love. The heat went through her skin and buried into her heart. Her breath caught, as she was overwhelmed by a feeling of joy and ecstasy.

Images flashed in her mind. There was a brilliantly blue sky with a large yellow sun. It cast golden rays down onto the earth below. One of the rays casted onto a wagon train, exactly like hers. A line ran down the middle, and two armies stood on either side. They wore leather armor and brandished swords. Men and women on both sides had faces of rage, and were ready to run at the other side.

But they stopped and stared as a woman walked down the middle divide. It was Sonja in a beautiful white dress. Around her were her friends Roose and Teresa, but not Britta. Her two friends were wearing orange robes, and held yellow flowers in their hands. Vision Sonja looked towards her friends, and they looked towards her, smiling. When they smiled the Sonja who was seeing this felt that deep sense of love within her. Vision Sonja walked towards the middle of the wagon train, past the yellow wood pews, towards the Keeper's wagon. On the podium stood Sigrun, also dressed in white. Sigrun had a smile of pure joy. Vision Sonja ran up the podium, and the two of them kissed.

When they kissed there was an explosion of

pure white light. All the people in the wagon train bowed their heads, and dropped their swords. They clapped and cheered, crossing the divide in the middle and hugging one another. Sonja and Sigrun turned towards these people, smiling, and putting their hands up in a regal manner. They both said, "We will lead you now."

Sonja was back in the Keeper's wagon. The wood around looked blurry. The Sol Shard felt hot in her hands. She looked down at it in wonder.

For a Keeper, getting a vision from Sol was rare. She was taught that only a handful ever got a vision: Keeper Isabelle who was given the vision of Sol coming back in the sky which was the foundation for the Mission, Keeper Aurora who had a vision of raiders killing every faithful so taught them how to fight and defend themselves, and her mother who had a vision about the decadence of the wagon train so brought in the focus on purity. Despite her belief, Sonja had never known whether these visions were true or not but now she had no doubt.

And she knew exactly what the vision was saying. She had been tasked to bring together the two sides of the wagon train. No longer should the religious side and the workers fight and fear each other. They should live in harmony. And she would do this by looking at the example of her friends, they were all different people and had different opinions but they seemed to be able to come together with love for each other. Having a sense of community and having a shared goal seemed key.

As for Sigrun, well the vision seemed to confirm that her feelings were not wrong. That if she embraced what she was and what she wanted then she could be accepted as a leader. And maybe if the two of them came together it would make the coming together of the wagon train more likely. Sonja did seem to remember that Sigrun said that she was going to be the new Jarl. Maybe if they were brought into union that would bring the faith and wagon train into union.

But she felt she was getting ahead of herself. She didn't really know Sigrun, and while she found her attractive she didn't know enough of her personality to know if they could really be together. Maybe it would happen, and that would be nice, but she felt the most important thing to do was to bring the people of the wagon train together.

And she felt the easiest way to do that was to

start with the ones that had been close but had drifted away. She was going to have a talk with the farmers.

***

Sigrun entered Bonde Square at break time. The sky was gray and heavy, with a light rain pattering down. The workers huddled around the awnings of wagons or covered their heads with cloaks, if they had them.

Yael had given her a new green cloak, fastened with a fancy brooch with her family's rune on, along with a new set of tunics and trousers. She had been very impressed that his workers had managed to make them so fast, as it had only been a few days since she had been named Jarl. When she had mentioned that, Yael had laughed and told her that if something was made a priority they could make it within a day if needs be.

With the cloak on she couldn't help but feel a little gaudy and elevated beyond her station. She still felt that the worn down, muddy tunic, with holes in them, was the garb that most suited her. But she guessed that she had to project the image of leadership and nobility to others.

Still, when she walked into Bonde Square she avoided being seen by Sven and some of the other Baldurs. They would spy on her and tell Gregor what she was asking. And she needed to keep her inquiries to herself for the moment. She didn't know why Gregor and Yael had lied about Hannes but if they did they would surely not be happy with her digging into it.

She went straight to a group of farmers that all stood under an awning. She greeted them and told them to carry on chatting. They eyed her a little suspiciously.

"It's kind of a shame that you don't see many Priestesses over here anymore," a thin man said, leaning back on the wagon. "Even though they wore their robes all across their bodies they were quite nice to look at."

"I heard that they were banned from having sex," a younger man to the side of the group said.

"Now that's definitely cruel," a woman with thick arms said.

"You wouldn't be able to survive, the amount you have, Aina," Thin Man said, looking at the rest of the men in the group and grinning.

"Hey I like to have my fun, definitely more fun than my hand, Thore," Aina replied.

This got a lot of 'oohs' and laughs from the group. Thore took the humor well and nodded his head in respect.

"What do you think this new Keeper is like?" Sigrun asked.

"I think only the bosses have interacted with her," Thore said. "From what they have been muttering, the Keeper hasn't really spent much time outside her wagon. When they ask the other faithful they say she is reading the scrolls."

"Man, I wish I could spend all day reading," Aina said.

"And miss all this great mud and dirt, nah," Thore replied, which got a few laughs from the group. There was a little bit of silence, as people shifted and thought about what to say next.

Sigrun got in there first. "And what about this new Jarl, what do you think about her?"

She couldn't deny she felt slightly strange asking the question, pretending that she wasn't the Jarl, but it was useful to get a real reaction from the people. Generally people didn't tell you their true opinion of their leaders, fearing retribution, or even just embarrassment. Sigrun felt that as she became more known, more and more would just be polite to her and it'd be hard to get the true reflection of her popularity. Now, when no one knew who she was, she could get a true assessment.

Thore shook his head. "I still don't get why Hannes was voted out by the council. I know they all keep saying that he would have made us starve to death, but I don't believe that. We have plenty of food and when we don't we just trade for it anyway."

"Yeah," Aina said, wistfully. "I liked Hannes."

"He did throw some great parties," Sigrun said.

Aina gave her a questioning look. "We liked him for more than just his parties. There was something about him, he seemed to get us, talk on our level. A lot of Jarls look down on us, see us as nobodies, he didn't."

"Plus you knew that he wouldn't give in to the Mission," a female voice in the group said. "He was going to go against them every step of the way. No wonder they voted him out."

"Well he still might be going against the Mission," the young man said, eyes bright. "With the…"

He was silenced with an elbow from Thore. "No talking about that stuff in front of newbies, Daniel"

Sigrun wondered what Daniel was going to say, surely it would have revealed in some way the true reason why Hannes had been voted out. "Come on, I'd love to know what you mean. I don't have any love for the Mission."

Thore narrowed his eyes. "You have a fancy cloak on and some nice clothes, we know you're one of the higher ups, so you'll have to forgive us if we don't share."

She could feel the rest of the group staring at her, and now becoming more guarded about their words. Damn it, and she was so close!

She nodded. "Fair enough, I think I've had enough fun for one afternoon."

Sigrun looked around to see if there were any other groups she could join. It felt like break time was winding down as a few people in the groups were waving their hands and walking away. The same thing was happening to this group, until an older man ran towards them.

"The Keeper, she's here," he shouted to them.

Despite their talk about disliking the Mission, everyone was interested in going to see the new Keeper. Sigrun was amongst them. She wanted to know whether it really was the same Sonja that had randomly kissed her.

She followed the group of farmers, as they joined the gathering crowd, and made their way to the entrance to Blomst Street.

A woman in an orange robe came walking through the square. As soon as Sigrun saw her, her heart beat fast and her mind went back to the passionate kiss on Kveg Plain. She knew exactly who the orange robed woman was, because that face had been in her dreams every night since she saw it. It *was* Sonja.

***

Sonja couldn't be anonymous anymore. As soon as she stepped out of the Keeper's wagon, the faithful formed a crowd. Men and women looked up and praised her, even though she hadn't said or done anything. It felt strange and wrong to get this amount of respect from them for just a title. Say what you will about her mother but she had at least shaped the Mission and had given it a direction that could be praised. Sonja hadn't even started any of her changes. She wondered whether she would still be praised by these faithful when she did.

The crowds were worse when within the wider

wagon train. Many stared at her, or formed a line, as she passed down Blomst Street. Despite the gray clouds overhead, the waft of perfume from the flowers gave everything a sense of spring. She could imagine that at any moment Manang would pop out of the clouds, and give everything a ray of red light.

The faces on the men and women that watched her were more mixed than the ones on the faithful. There were some that looked at her in wonder and respect, but most had neutral faces, silently judging whether they should like her or not. Though she noticed that a few in the back had very hostile faces. What surprised her about that was that those hostile faces still stood to see her. She would have thought that if they had hated her they would just not show up. But she guessed that even amongst the workers the title of Keeper had a fascination to it. Even if you hated it, you still had to see who was using it, so at least you could know the face you would be hating from now on.

As Sonja walked past the wagons in Blomst Street - with baskets of flowers hung on their front axles - a little girl ran out in front of her. Sonja stopped, and bent down to the girl. The girl had striking red hair and a bright happy face. Her hand held a single red rose, which she proffered to Sonja. Sonja thanked her and delicately took the rose, bowing her head. The crowd cheered and clapped, and even the faces that had been hostile a moment ago broke out in slight smiles.

She felt an important moment had just happened, that she had in a small way shown everyone what kind of Keeper she would be. In her bones she felt that her mother would have never acknowledged the little girl or taken her gift. Her mother would have looked down at the girl, seen her as impure and not worthy enough for her attention. That was why Sonja felt that a lot of the caravan was against the faith. The crowd thought that people like her thought they were better than them, and forced them to become better by trying to change the laws.

Sonja understood deep down that she was not better than the people, in some ways she was worse. She didn't feel that everyone ate or drank excessively, or paid for sex. She needed them to understand that she was on the same level as them, and by doing that she could then say "hey let's become better together." Not in the extreme pure way that her mother had demanded, just in a way that brought the people into a unified community.

She had to stop when she entered Bonde Square, as the crowd had circled around the exit from Blomst Street. All these farmers looked up at her, pleading for something. At first she didn't really know what to do, what could she give these people that would please them? But then she flashed back to her mother in a similar situation within the faith, how she would loom over people, give the Sol sign, and say a little prayer. She decided to do the same. When she told them they were blessed by Sol, many had tears in their eyes and thanked her profusely.

As she passed each worker, she became more and more confident at making the Sol sign and saying a prayer. Every time a person would thank her she would get a boost of joy, and smile. She might actually be changing these people's lives, even just a little.

When she got into the middle of the crowd she stopped dead. Sonja recognized the face staring at her instantly. She had seen it in her dreams every night since they had kissed. Though the Sigrun in front of her now was wearing completely different clothes, a finely made tunic with cloak. Clearly Sigrun hadn't joked about becoming Jarl.

"Would you also like a prayer, Jarl," she said,

trying to keep her voice serene even though her heart was beating like mad.

There were a few gasps and mutterings from some of the men and women that surrounded Sigrun when she said the words Jarl. Sigrun grimaced, and looked back at them in an apologetic manner.

"No I don't need a prayer," Sigrun said. "But it's good to see the new Keeper. I feel we should meet some time. Have a chat about the wagon train and how we see our roles within it."

Sonja's breath caught. She had wanted to meet Sigrun ever since they had met, but she had just not had the courage to go find her. However was Sigrun inviting her now for personal reasons, or just because she was the faith's leader?

"I would like that, do you feel it should be in your wagon or in mine?" she said, hating that everyone was looking on at them, scrutinizing everything they were saying.

"I think my wagon might be more comfortable for a meeting, though I will confess I am not familiar with your wagon," Sigrun said.

It might have been Sonja's imagination but it felt that Sigrun was putting a flirtatious spin on her words. Sigrun was staring at her with come hither eyes, that Sonja hoped no one else could recognize.

"You are probably right, most of my wagon is made of candles and scrolls. If we want a chat I'm sure you have better facilities for it."

Sigrun bowed. "I look forward to meeting you. Shall we say after whatever you are doing here?"

"Yes!"

Sonja's heart pounded, she wanted to go back with Sigrun now, but she came here for a reason. And since the crowd had already gathered, she might as well say that reason now.

"I have come to you here to start something special. I believe that after your harvest you workers have a little celebration. Me and my faithful would like to host that celebration. Bring whatever you were going to bring to your celebration to ours, and yes that does include drink."

There were a few chuckles, and some gasps from that. Everyone knew that the faithful didn't usually allow drinking or excessive eating, so for her to be suggesting to do both was a big thing.

This was what Sonja was hoping for. She would show the wagon train that the faithful were different, or at least they would be under her leadership.

TWO LOVERS MEET ON THE RIVER OF LIFE

'Two Lovers Meet' Skald Song

Sigrun kept re-arranging everything in the Jarl's wagon in preparation for Sonja's visit. Everything had to be comfortable and perfect for her. Initially Sigrun was going to keep everything in the room the same. Her and Sonja would sit in the armchairs at the desk, Sigrun sitting behind it and Sonja in front, but she felt that was way too formal. Then she decided to take the armchair behind the desk and moved it to the front, but when she sat down to test it she felt the desk got in the way. Finally she decided to move the desk, but then realised there would be nothing to put any drinks down on.

Should she serve drinks? Sigrun remembered that the Mission was pretty against drinking and drunkenness, so she felt offering the leader of the faith one might be insulting. But then again Sonja did say to the workers they could bring drinks to the harvest party, so did that mean she was pro drinking? In the end Sigrun decided to move the small circular bed stand next to the armchairs, and put a bottle of whiskey and two glasses on it just in case.

Next she stoked the fire, so the room would be warm and cozy, and neatened her mother's books on the shelf. Even with everything major done, she still felt she couldn't just sit and wait for Sonja. She paced across the room, neatening up the silk curtain hanging from the four-poster bed, straightening the Kings Game on the desk, checking the bottle of whiskey for the hundredth time, and shifting the chairs a few millimeters so they were in the right optimal place.

Her heart was beating like mad, and her brain thought of a hundred different worries. What if she got the tone of their meeting wrong and this was actually a political meeting and not a date, what if Sonja got to know her and she didn't like the real her, what if Sonja found her uncouth and vulgar? Now part of Sigrun didn't want Sonja to knock on the door, just so these things wouldn't happen.

The knock on the door came. Sigrun almost ran to the door to open it, but understood at the last second that she couldn't seem that desperate. She brushed her hair back, shifted her tunic a little, and opened the door.

Manang had come out of the clouds at the

perfect moment, because when she opened the door Sonja was bathed in a brilliant glow of red light. Her robes radiated a burst of flame orange, which complemented the redness of Sonja's cheeks. Her hair seemed to counterpoint it all, the dark black absorbing the light.

Seeing Sonja smiling and holding herself up like a leader caught Sigrun's breath. She just stared at her dumbly, all sense of politeness gone out of the window. However Sonja took it in her stride, nodding to Sigrun, and closing the door behind her.

She closed out any prying eyes that had found themselves gathered around the Jarl's wagon.

Sigrun got back her composure and the job that she had to do. She gestured to the armchair. "Welcome Keeper, it's a pleasure to meet you…err…again."

Sonja smiled at this, and sat down at the armchair. "You can forget all the formalities. We are alone together. No one outside can see or hear this."

Sigrun breathed a sigh of relief, so this was something more than a political meeting. She sat down and grabbed the bottle of whiskey. "Do you want some?"

"Yes," Sonja said.

Sigrun poured out a good two shots of whiskey in each glass. Her hands were shaking. "I'm kind of surprised you are drinking, and told the farmers that they could drink. I thought drinking was banned in the faith."

"It is," Sonja said, taking a good glug of the whiskey. "But I hope to change that whole purity nonsense."

Sigrun looked surprised. "I thought that nonsense was your whole thing."

"It was my Mother's thing. You can't eat meat, you can't drink at all." Sonja shook her head. "It just alienated everyone in the wagon train."

"So the previous Keeper was your Mother?" She asked.

"Not my true mother. She adopted me and a few others. But I guess in a way since she was the one that brought me up and taught me everything I knew, and apparently loved me dearly despite it all, she is as true a mother as you can get."

"How young were you when you were adopted? Do you remember what it was like before?"

"Enough to know how horrible it was," Sonja said, draining her glass. "Anyway this is not the fun conversation I was hoping to get from you."

Sigrun raised her eyebrows. "Is that something you wanted?"

Sonja grabbed the bottle and poured another glass. "It's just that I don't want to remember back then, it was horrible, and whatever else my Mother did, I am eternally grateful that she saved me from it and put me on a different path."

"I'm not going to force you to say anything you don't want. But I will say, for some weird reason I want to get to know you more than have fun with you," Sigrun said, sipping on her drink. "Like I'm not going to lie, I've had many casual flings with a lot of women, and those usually start with fun and flirty conversations. But for you…that feels wrong."

"I understand, I didn't actually mean it, I feel the same way. You might not know this but my relationships with women have mostly been…transactional."

Sonja looked down at the ground in shame. Sigrun didn't totally know what she was ashamed of, but she could guess. The faith had told her that who she loved was wrong in some way. She leant forward and held Sonja's hand.

"You have nothing to be ashamed of."

Sonja glanced up at her. "Are you sure about

that? What if I told you that all my relationships with women were paid for?"

"Getting paid, damn I should have thought of that."

Sonja laughed, and took a sip of her drink.

The two of them were still holding hands. Neither of them moved away from each other, it seemed that they both wanted to stay there, feeling each other. Unfortunately, Sigrun had drunk all her whiskey. She didn't want to break the embrace, but her mouth had gone very dry and she felt very nervous all of a sudden. She wasn't usually nervous when speaking to a woman, could even say she was way too forward when it came to pursuing what she wanted, but for Sonja it was different. Sigrun wanted Sonja to not be put off of her.

She unclasped her hands and picked up the whiskey bottle. The two of them sat back, but there was a change in the air, like they had gotten closer in some way.

The two sipped their drinks, staring at each other. Neither of them spoke or made another move. It felt like a dance where they didn't totally know the positions they needed to be in or the flow of the music. Should they talk more, or should they do what they wanted to do deep down: kiss passionately.

Sonja was the one to break the silence. "Do you believe in Sol?"

"I used to, but not much anymore. There was a time that I prayed for Sol but she did not answer."

Now it was her turn to not want to think about the past negatively. But Sonja seemed to understand the hurt that lay behind her words, as she asked. "Did something horrible happen that Sol did nothing about?"

Sigrun nodded. "How do you know?"

"As a Priestess I had to stand in various market squares telling everyone how wonderful Sol was and how she would eventually appear in the sky. Most ignored us, but there were a few that got really angry at us, like getting in your face almost ready to punch you anger. At first I didn't understand it, but then I started to internalize what they shouted at me. They would shout about how they prayed for their son to get better but Sol never healed them, how they prayed to have a better marriage or to find someone special but it never materialized. Usually people just live their life thinking Sol exists, but the ones that truly go against the idea, the ones that have no faith or truly hate it, are the ones that have had some kind of tragedy or sadness in their lives that Sol failed to prevent."

"It was my mother," Sigrun said, softly. "She had some kind of disease that no one knew how to cure. I remember in the last days she was lying in bed, her face gaunt, and the smell was as if a dead cow was still in the stables." She drank her glass of whiskey, feeling a dull pain inside. "I remember every night seeing her get weaker and weaker, praying to Sol to get rid of that illness, desperately crying out for her to heal her. But she never did, and my mother died."

Sonja leant over, and held Sigrun's hand again. It felt soft, comforting. Even though her glass was empty again, she didn't want to break away from that embrace.

"I mean, I'm sorry to say, but what's the point of your faith if Sol can't affect things?" Sigrun said, bitterly. "She isn't in the sky, she's dead even by your reckoning, so I get that she can't really be here to do everything. But isn't her being dead the same as if she doesn't exist? Why do you pray to her, and fight for her?"

Sonja gazed into her eyes. "I feel that she does affect things, but since she isn't in the sky anymore it can only be small. I feel in my heart that she brought my mother into the town I was in to adopt me. Sol nudges us down paths, shows us the true ways of things, gives us a purpose in life."

"I've been wanting a purpose in my life for some time. I can't deny that I've felt empty and despondent in the last few months. Parties and drinking just doesn't feel that void."

"Yes you are right, drinking doesn't fulfill you. But I wouldn't get rid of parties, if done right they bring people together. That's what my Mission wants to do, unify people."

"I'm afraid I just can't be in your Mission. They would hate what I am, what I do."

Sonja squeezed her hand. "If they knew about me, what I'm doing now, they would hate it. They would exile me in an instant. I hope to change that, maybe then you might be confident enough to join."

Sigrun gazed into Sonja's eyes, seeing how serious she was. It didn't make any sense why Sonja was within a faith that hated her, but she did know that if anyone would change their attitude it would be her.

As she gazed into Sonja's brown eyes, her heart

beat faster and faster. A desire rushed through her veins. She leant over, and kissed Sonja.

It was as electrifying and passionate as it had been when they first met, maybe even more so. Sigrun leaned into it, grabbing hold of Sonja. She wanted to take off that robe, fling her onto the bed.

Sonja pushed her away.

Sigrun lay back, a little confused and hurt. Sonja was catching her breath. "It's not that I don't want it…it just can't be now.""Why not?"

"Because many people saw me come into your wagon and I think they'll expect me to come out again. And I'm not doing some quick thing with you. I'm done with transactional love."

Sigrun understood, but still felt crushed and disappointed. "When will we see each other again, when will we be able to…spend the night. Isn't this always going to be a problem that people might see us or find out?"

Sonja looked at her sadly. "Maybe, but I want to be with you so I want to try to make it work. Maybe we will just have to sneak around at night for a bit. But I promise that I will change my Mission enough that they will accept who I love, and then we can be out in the open."

"I look forward to that day," Sigrun said, getting up and brushing her hair back.

She helped Sonja up from the armchair. The two of them stood close to one another awkwardly. Sigrun's heart was telling her to kiss her again, and be damned with the consequences, but she didn't want to go against Sonja's wishes. If they were going to have a good relationship Sigrun would need to respect her wishes, even if they pained her.

In the end, she hugged Sonja. "I will be counting down the days until I see you again."

Sonja beamed. "I will be doing the same. I believe that Sol will allow me to see you soon."

"Can you refer me to her, cause I'd like to book tomorrow night if possible."

Sonja laughed, which brought joy in Sigrun's heart, one that she hadn't felt since her mother had been alive.

Sonja opened the door, gave her one final look, and stepped outside. The door closed, and Sigrun was left on her own, feeling the sense of joy and excitement but also feeling a deep sense of sadness as well. She sat down, and finished the last drops of the whiskey bottle.

Part Two

Build Up Of Light

CAST THE TORCH WITHIN TO BANISH YOUR OWN SHADOW

'Scroll of Commandment'

After the get-together with Sigrun, Sonja walked back into the Mission enclave in a daze again. All her mind, body, and heart thought about Sigrun's face, her blond hair, her earthy smell. She wanted to go back to feel that hair, inhale that smell. It felt like her whole body was screaming to get more, but she couldn't follow it.

Priestesses and Priests watched her as walked. All her movements were observed by the faithful and the non faithful alike. Every time she said something or did something people would talk about it. If she went back to the Jarl's wagon again, spent the night with Sigrun, than they would know about her being gay. She felt that the faith wouldn't be able to handle that. She had to change it.

The deeper Sonja walked the more of a crowd gathered around. Many faithful seemed to want the same as the farmers in Bonde Square: the sign of Sol, and a prayer. Sonja wondered how her mother lived having to do this everyday, but she remembered that for the most part her mother didn't come out of the Keeper's wagon and when she did she had a few Priestesses guarding her and moving the crowd along. Maybe she should get some bodyguards?

After the tenth Sol sign and prayer, she was glad that the next people to come up to her were her three friends. But her happiness was tempered by the fact they looked at her with concern.

"What is wrong," she asked.

"Are the rumors true?" Britta said, furrowing her brow.

Sonja's heart leaped for a second, had people figured out what had happened between her and Sigrun? "What rumors?"

"That you told the farmers they could have a party here, with alcohol," Britta replied, putting as much disdain on the last words as she could.

Sonja sighed with relief. "Yes I did say that, and I will tell the faithful why."

Britta looked confused. "Partying and drinking is against our teachings, what are you doing?"

Sonja glanced at her other friends. Roose had concern on her face, while Teresa was glancing between her and Britta like she wasn't too sure who she should pick. She had to be delicate here, she didn't want to lose her friends.

"I feel it might be best if I explain it to everyone. But after I do, you can come to me in the wagon and we can discuss your individual concerns."

Britta looked like she wanted to say more, but she nodded her head. The three of them turned around and melted back into the crowd. Sonja felt a little uneasy with how furious Britta seemed about letting farmers drink. What if the other faithful would be like that? What if her mother had drilled the idea of extreme purity in so much that even the idea of a party full of drinking was too much for them. If they couldn't handle that they definitely wouldn't be able to handle her feelings for women. What if she was just doing all this work for nothing?

She shook her head, at least she had to try before being exiled. Even if it didn't work at least she could put her head up high and say she had a go.

She told the crowd that she would be speaking at the Keeper's wagon, and that they should gather the rest of the faithful. The crowd dispersed quickly, which gave her a few moments of peace and quiet. She walked past the training grounds, a large cart full of gravel, with poles in the centre to attack. A few Priestesses were training their sword skills, making quick strikes at the pole. Sonja couldn't help but look at them like she had in the past, she loved to look at women moving their muscles and making a sweat. But instead of looking at the Priestesses that were training now, she imagined Sigrun in their place. She imagined Sigrun's thick arms holding a sword, striking fast, looking back at her smiling.

A heat rose up in Sonja's face, and she strode across the grass to cool off. Was this what the other women felt like in their relationships with men? Was she in love?

Thankfully there were a few yellow robed Priest's and Priestesses sat at the pews to distract her from her feelings towards Sigrun. She had to be focused in this speech, she couldn't have an image of Sigrun popping into her head distracting her. This speech would be the first test of whether she could really be a Keeper that changed the faith.

The Priests and Priestesses stood up and bowed. She gave them the Sol sign and nodded her head. She walked through the pews, and ascended the stairs to the podium. She waited, looking out at the seats that were slowly being filled by the faithful. All the men and women who sat down looked up at her in awe and expectation, it felt familiar to the stares she had when her name had been announced as Keeper. She had to close her eyes and banish the feeling of wanting to run away again.

She focused instead of what she was going to say. What was she telling the faithful, how would she make them understand that purity was a harmful force for them? The answer that came to her, like a light that shone from the Sol Shard, was to reveal her struggles. Not all of them, she didn't feel the faithful could accept all of her at the moment, but enough to make them understand that their Keeper wasn't the perfect pure person they thought she was.

Soon the pews were filled up with Priests, Priestesses, and Acolytes. Her friends sat at the front. Roose and Teresa looked up at her in the same way the others did, full of awe and respect, but Britta brows were furrowed and her arms were folded. It looked like it would take some convincing for her to get on board. Sonja hoped that she could.

A silence fell over the crowd, the wind blew

through grass and the wagons creaked. Sonja felt her heart beat faster and her mouth go dry. She coughed, and began.

"First of all I'd like to apologize for not doing this sooner. I really should have come up on this podium the first day I was named and show what the faith would be like with me as Keeper. But the reason I didn't do that, the reason I ran away instead was because I was troubled."

There were a few murmurs of confusion and shock at that statement. Most Keepers didn't highlight their troubles and flaws, most just talked about the importance of unity and how they saw the faith going forwards.

"The reason why I ran away is because I didn't feel worthy of the title. My mother was a great Keeper to all of you, she strengthened this faith and gave you all a purpose and a goal in life, how could anyone follow that? But that isn't the true reason why I felt I didn't deserve it, you would understand that, maybe some of you even thought that was the case, and when I came back you pushed it out of your minds, something that could be forgiven. No, the real reason I didn't feel worthy is because I felt I was too full of shadow."

Now there were audible gasps from the crowd.

No one admitted their shadow out loud, no one admitted they had any shadow because they had to be seen to be pure. A normal Keeper might have paused at this, felt they had gone too far, but Sonja had wanted this, had wanted to shock them a little. Through that shock, she could change their viewpoints. She became confident and sure of her speech.

"Yes, I am full of shadow. I didn't like to admit it, in fact I felt ashamed about it, but I cannot deny it is a part of me. You see when I was a teenager I heard about the feasts and the dancing, and I wanted to go. Maybe many of you have felt that same urge, well the difference is I acted upon it. One night I tiptoed out of the wagon and found one of these parties. I let loose, drinking, eating, and dancing as much as I could. But some of you might just chalk that up to being a teenager, wanting to sample the delights of shadow before going on the path of the light. I'm afraid, however, it didn't stop at just one party."

"Every month or so I would sneak out of the wagon and enjoy the delights of those parties. Whenever we would go to a new town and city I would try to find their gatherings. In the moment of drinking and dancing I felt free, it felt like I had broken away from a prison. But the morning after

I felt ashamed. The things I was doing at those parties were the exact things that the faith, my mother, said were wrong. I tried to be better, I tried to push those feelings out of my system. Sometimes I would succeed, going two months maybe even three without partying, but I would always succumb in the end. That feeling of freedom was just too intoxicating, too joyous."

Sonja could see that many of the faces in the crowd had become either confused or shocked. She glanced at Britta, who had such fury on her face that she faltered in her speech for a moment. There was a deep dark feeling inside that told her that when she finished this speech, her and Britta would no longer be friends.

She breathed in and rallied herself, this was more important than their relationship. This was to change the faith, to allow her to be the person she always was.

"Now you may be wondering why I'm speaking to you about this, some of you may think that because of this shadow that I do not deserve to be Keeper. Well this is exactly what I felt when I ran away. But the reason why I came back, and the reason I accepted being Keeper, is that I had the sudden realization that my feelings were not wrong. Now yes, I can admit that I gave into my desires too many times, but I don't think the desires was wrong."

"For what does Keeper Isabelle say in the Scroll of Foundation: 'I saw a giant yellow sun in the sky, and it shone down below on a magnificent garden. The trees were leafy and vibrantly green, and their bark was a deep brown. Birds fluttered within branches, and small animals rushed within the similarly vibrant green grass. Many of my faithful were within this garden, sitting on benches. They held mugs of ale, and feasted on a wide range of food. They seemed to beckon me inwards. When I did the person next to me said that this was all given to them by Sol, that now Sol was back in the sky the earth was a paradise, and that they could enjoy themselves with ale and food forever.'"

"Does this passage not say that when Sol comes back in the sky that we will enjoy feasting and drinking? Why then do we deny ourselves the pleasure of those things now? Sol wants us to be happy in that garden, so what's wrong with having that happiness now?"

"Yes I have read the other passages, especially Priest Robin's account, and understand how it talks about the dangers of overeating, how it can lead to starvation, and the dangers of drinking too much, how it can lead to fights and babies out of wedlock, but just because there are these dangers doesn't mean eating and drinking is bad."

"For you see, when I went to those parties and ate that food I connected to the people within those parties. I became friends with some of them, and through these friendships they began to understand me and I began to understand them. What a powerful way to bring the Mission into people's lives. For if they begin to understand us, they will begin to understand why we follow the faith of Sol. By doing that we can bring moderation. No more will there be parties every week, feasts that will starve us, and drunken excesses. Instead there will be parties that celebrate something, a chance to get together and learn about one another, a chance to unite the wagon train.

"Our purity drive has alienated others. Sure we can sit on our pedestal basking in the glow of our perfection, but by doing that we are failing in our Mission. Many in our own wagon train hate us, want to get rid of us. These are our neighbors, these are the ones following us on the Mission. If we cannot convince them to join us, then we cannot convince anyone else. Our drive to purity has alienated them, but I also fear it is alienating ourselves.

"I truly felt like I wanted to quit the faith because I wanted that prison of needing to be pure to be gone. I was willing to throw it all away for parties and food, just because I didn't want to feel that shame again. Maybe it's just me who felt that, but I don't think so. I bet there are many young acolytes who feel ashamed about their inner feelings, I bet there are many Priests and Priestesses who on occasions do shadow things. This is not healthy and it will destroy us. I am here to change all that."

"I am changing both by setting up a harvest festival for the farmers. This will be a chance to get to know our fellows, the ones that have supported us throughout the life of the wagon train. I have felt that even these people have drifted away, not seeing them at prayers or get-togethers anymore. We need to strengthen that bond again, and if we do that then we will know we can do the same for the others. I truly believe in the dream of a united wagon train. I hope you can follow in that dream."

Sonja finished, feeling hoarse and exhausted

from all that speaking. She looked out at the crowd of faithful, wondering what they would think of her speech. Everyone was silent, the men and women in the crowd had furrowed brows and seemed to be thinking. Sonja's heart pounded more and more. She could have handled angry boos, but silence seemed to be the worst response.

But there was movement on the front pew. Teresa stood up, and clapped. Soon Roose joined in, and so did others behind them. One by one all the faithful were standing up and clapping. Some started to woop and shout out her name. Sonja felt a sense of relief.

The only thing that marred that was the fact that Britta was sitting there with her arms crossed, looking like she wanted to kill Sonja.

IT'S EASY TO GET PEOPLE ON YOUR SIDE: JUST THROW A LOT OF PARTIES, TELL THEM HOW GREAT YOU'LL MAKE THEIR LIVES, AND GIVE THEM A PURPOSE

'Diary of the King's Skald' by Alf Beumers

Sigrun was uncomfortable sleeping in her new comfy bed. It somehow felt wrong not having weird lumps in the mattress, and rigidity at her back. Her spine was being absorbed in the bed, which caused twinging and pain. The Jarl's wagon was way too hot. What was cozy and pleasant during the day felt stifling underneath the covers. The silk curtains around her bed unnerved her a little as well. The room beyond looked like it swam in a silver mug of beer. She had gotten used to being able to see her own door at all times, knowing that she would be able to spot any intruder coming in.

She sighed, and pushed the curtains away. Everything in the Jarl's wagon was dim and shadowy. There were only black silhouettes of the armchairs and desk. Nothing stirred, not even a creak. She had gotten too used to the sounds of cows sleeping and the gentle creak of the wood.

This wagon was too quiet.

For Sigrun everything felt too new. There was no familiar anchor she could take comfort in, until she saw her mother's books. She walked over to the shelf and took down *'How Manang Ate The Sun'*. The thought of her mother's voice would comfort and soothe her. But when she sat down in the armchair and went to read, she found it hard to concentrate. Her mind refused to let the meanings of the words sink in, instead it thought about Sonja.

Sonja had been in her thoughts all day. Whenever she would be walking in the wagon train Sonja's flame robe would appear in the corner of her eye, whenever she would be speaking to a caravaner Sonja's sultry stare would be looking back at her. At inappropriate times, when she was talking with a higher up Baldur or Hoademaker, she would think about what Sonja looked like under those faithful robes. She felt heat around her neck and face, which made her excuse herself from the wagon to get some air.

What had Sonja done to her? Was this what people felt in relationships? Was she in love?

She shook her head, pushing herself up from the armchair. She had to see Sonja. Sigrun didn't care that it was the dead of night and Sonja was sleeping in the middle of the faithful encampment.

In her younger days there were many times she would have to sneak in or out of wagons. This one time she had flirted with a cute redhead at a party, and when the redhead took Sigrun back to her wagon Sigrun found that she had to tiptoe around the redhead's family sleeping on the floor. On the plus side due to circumstances of not wanting to wake up the family the sex with her had been slow and sensual.

Sigrun slipped into her boots, and opened the door. She stepped onto the grass, and quickly ran over to wagons that ringed around the faithful encampment. She peered through the alleyway, seeing if there were any faithful about. Only the grass within the encampment and the dirt on the training ground blew in the wind. Crouching down, she rushed down the alleyway and ran out into the open grass.

At first she thought she was safe, but then a yellow light flashed in the corner of her eye. Her heart beat fast, and she ran back to the alleyway. She put her back onto the side of the wagon, peering around the corner. The light initially blinded her, but soon the silhouette of a person was visible. Sigrun ran back out of the alleyway.

She stopped just outside to catch her breath, seeing the yellow light pass the position she had just stood. She had gotten lucky. If the guard had caught her, she would have had no clue what excuse she would have for going into the faith's encampment at the dead of night. Her actions would have gotten to Sonja, and Sonja would be disappointed about it and a little wary of her doing it again.

Her actions had been very stupid. She slinked back to the Jarl's wagon, feeling a little embarrassed.

When she clenched the wagon's silver doorknob and looked through the frosted glass, she didn't feel like opening the door. The night's cool air had awakened her, and she felt a little lonely. The only thing in the wagon for her were dark armchairs and an uncomfortable bed. She wondered whether there was a party she could go to instead. At a party she could drink her embarrassment and sorrows away, and dance to forget Sonja for a bit.

At the thought of parties a memory popped into her head. She had been with that group of farmers with a thin man, a woman with thick arms, and the young farmer. The young farmer - was Daniel his name? - had been about to reveal how Hannes was still fighting the faith, but he had been prevented from saying it by the thin man, was his name Thore?.

Hannes had been throwing a lot of parties lately, one every week. Sigrun questioned why he had done that. It didn't make sense for him to just be doing it for the people to love him, making the stores empty that quickly was too risky a move for something as small as that. So there had to be something that Hannes was getting out of it. She flashed back to that note in the Jarls wagon, the one that talked about getting rid of the Mission of Sol. Was he organizing something?

She wondered if whatever Hannes was organizing would be on tonight. She didn't want to go back to her wagon, and she couldn't see Sonja, so maybe she should try to find out.

Sigrun started exploring the wagon train to see if she could find any tell-tale runes or random bits of furniture, usually these would indicate a party or a get together. Despite parties not being outlawed, people tried to hide them so budding faithful didn't come around to proselytize. She started on the west side of the wagon train, the

Mattsons' side. She walked down Rod Street, crouching down to see the bottom corner of wagons or their axles. Sigrun didn't find anything on either side of the street.

She walked into Mattsons' Square, looking down each street. There was a table and chairs down Fregne Street, but when she looked closer there were just cards and half drunk beer on the table, and the chairs looked like they had just been pushed out of the way so people could get up.

Sigrun walked down the street anyway, just in case, and turned onto Slakter Row. Here the metallic smell of animal blood still permeated the air. The wagons down here were made out of rough metal, which looked sharp and foreboding in the night. All of Sigrun's cows - though she guessed they weren't her cows anymore - would eventually be transported into one of these wagons to be slaughtered. She understood it was for the good of the wagon train, and she enjoyed the meat that came from the cows, but she couldn't help still feel a little shudder down her spine. She shook out of her mind any imaginings of metal floors covered in cows blood.

She exited Slakter Row, and entered Bonde

Square. Here she checked the wagons forming the square, and then made her way to the carts full of dirt. There was no sign of any runes that indicated any parties or get-togethers.

The sky lightened to a muddy gray. It was becoming morning time faster than Sigrun had expected. Soon her chance of finding anything except for smoked out bonfires and stamped on grass was becoming more and more unlikely. She stood in the middle of the square, sighing. Hannes had done a good job in hiding his get-togethers, but there must be some way for people to know where it was being held.

She was about ready to give up until tomorrow night, when she heard the distant sound of voices. They were coming from the east, down Baldur Street. She ran towards a wagon at the edge of the street, putting her back towards the wood, and peered down.

Two men and one woman walked down the street. When Sigrun looked closer, she recognized the man in the middle as Thore, which must mean the other was Daniel, and that meant the woman was Aina. They all talked loudly.

"We are going to be late," Daniel said.

"Well we would have gotten there early if she

hadn't had to have a few drinks beforehand," Thore said, pointing to Aina. "I was willing to leave her in her stupor on the chair, but you insisted she had to come."

"It's always been the three of us," Daniel said. "Doesn't seem right not to take her."

"Well if Hannes gets us to carry everything or put things away, I know who I'm going to blame," Thore replied.

Sigrun waited until the three farmers walked further down the street, and then she followed them. She hugged the sides of the wagons, crouching and tiptoeing as she went. Anytime the group stopped and looked around, she sidled towards a wagon and froze. Her heart thumped, and she worried that she was going to get caught, but then the group would carry on.

Eventually they turned off the street and walked into a hidden square. Sigrun crouched down to the ground, and crawled underneath one of the wagons that formed it.

Inside the square nearly a hundred men and women stood in formation. Many wore the rough and muddy garb of farmers, but there were some in tailored tunics. The makeup of the formation had some black hair or chubby features, but the main bulk of it was made up of red haired men and women. Everyone held a sword in one hand and a shield in the other. They all looked forward, at poles that had been staked into the grass.

Standing in front of these poles was a tall, thin man, with brushed back blond hair. He had a bony face with a large forehead, and wore leather armor and thick trousers. Sigrun recognized him from the parties she had attended. He had always been in the middle of them, with an entourage of men and women at his side. He must have been Hannes.

The gathered men and women with swords looking like they were ready to enact violence made Sigrun uncomfortable, but what chilled her to the core was the fact that hanging on the poles was the yellow robes of the faithful.

Hannes' hard stare examined the men and women in formation. "Are you strong enough to charge at a group of Priests and Priestesses?"

The group shouted yes. Hannes stepped aside from the poles. "Well I want to see your best effort."

The men and women at the front of the formation cried out, running towards the poles. Their swords slashed in unison, and then it was the turn for the next line to attack. By the time the last row attacked the robes were in pieces on the floor.

Sigrun stared at the small pieces of cloth, imagining Sonja's wounded and bloody body in one of them. She gasped.

Hannes glanced towards her wagon. As he walked towards it, she scrambled back out. She pushed herself up and ran down the street, not looking back. Her mind raced.

The parties that Hannes had been throwing had really been a way to recruit people. He had been getting people together to drink and have fun, while he went around to talk to the ones that didn't like the faith. Hannes would then tell these people to come over to a secret square to teach them how to fight. And Hannes was teaching them how to fight and kill the faithful.

ONE OF THE MOST IMPORTANT ROLES FOR A KEEPER IS TO KEEP THE FAITH UNIFIED. YOU MUST KEEP ALL OF THE FAITHFUL ON ONE PATH

'Scroll of The Keeper'

Sonja expected the crowd of faithful outside her wagon to have disappeared the day after her speech. Most faithful would have followed Britta's anger about her proposals. Many would not want the faith to change and would be plotting her downfall. It would take her putting on a good harvest festival to change their minds even a little. This was not the case.

When she stepped down the stairs of the Keeper's wagon, Sonja found herself within a throng of faithful. They all gathered close, looking at her in awe, putting up their hands towards her, or shouting about how she was wonderful. Sonja had tried to get used to crowds, but this seemed to be an extra level of devotion that she wasn't prepared for. She felt a little weird, undeserving, and also slightly worried that one of the faithful would try to grab her and pull her in. She would really need to get some bodyguards soon.

Sonja tried to push through as quickly as possible, giving the Sol sign and a prayer, but not stopping. But then she saw the faces of awe anew. These people actually wanted to follow her new path, and thought it was a good thing. She let that sink in for a moment. It made her smile. Maybe changing the faith would be easier than she thought.

She was also struck by the fact that she had a willing body of workers. With their help she could make sure this harvest festival was as big and fun as it could be.

She stood up straight, glancing at the crowd around her. "My faithful, what a joy it is to see you all this morning, paying your respects to me."

All the men and women in the crowd bowed their heads and murmured their grateful thanks. At one level she still felt she didn't deserve all this praise, underneath everything there was still the shame of being shadow filled and not being her mother. But a new feeling crowded that out, one of pride and joy. She felt after all the time of feeling horrible about herself and wanting to exit the faith – whether that meant exile or death – that she deserved to be praised as someone of value. If her mother could feel like a royal leader and bask in the glory others gave her, why couldn't she?

"I said in my speech yesterday that I am hosting this year's harvest festival. That will mean we need to get everything ready. I want people to check how much food we have, how much seating we have, and where we can get some ale. I also want the training grounds moved, and tables, chairs, and a place to cook in its place." She clapped her hands. "Please go do that for me, my faithful."

As soon as she said the words the people of the crowd turned and ran to various different places to do the jobs she ordered. At the moment they all did it a little chaotically, some going into the store wagons, others grabbing chairs from wagons, some grabbing hold of the training ground. She made a note to talk to Teresa, Roose, and Sigmund to put some order to things.

She realized she hadn't placed Britta on that list. She felt a heavy weight around her heart at the thought of Britta being furious at her. She should try to talk to her, to get her on board.

Britta stood on the grass in the distance with a dozen other yellow robed men and women. They looked over to Sonja with stony faces. She sighed.

She would have to go over there and hear them out. But before she took one step, she heard a voice behind her.

"Keeper."

Sonja turned to see a girl looking up to her. She was about twelve years old, wearing white Acolyte robes. The girl had brown curly hair and a bright innocent face. She looked up at Sonja in awe, but there was also a tinge of sadness within.

"Yes, my child," Sonja said.

"I'd just like to say how important I found the speech you made yesterday," the girl said, the sadness in her eyes becoming greater.

"How so?" she asked, bending down so she was face to face with the girl. "And may I ask your name."

"Andrea," the innocent girl said. "And it was important to me because I've been feeling like I've been full of shadow myself. I always compare myself to the other acolytes and they seem to be purer than me. It just made me feel so horrible and ashamed."

"I know what you mean, I felt the same way. And may I ask what shadow you felt you had within you."

The little girl looked down at the ground,

squirming a little. Sonja put her arm on her shoulder. "You can tell me, I will not judge or exile you. Your secret is safe with me."

"I was starting to get noticed for looking at other girls. The other girls said it was to do with being gay and it was the gravest shadow they knew and that I should be exiled for it. I tried to defend myself, but I wondered if they were right. I wondered if I did have that shadow within. I wished I wouldn't have it if that was the case."

Sonja's heart beat. She had found another person within the faith like her, this was her chance to fix the things that had made her feel so miserable, at least for another child. Forget about the harvest festival and changing the minds of the wider faith, this was her most important action right here.

"I don't feel what you did is a shadow. Many girls look at boys the same way and we don't punish it, because they say that's more natural. But I would say looking at others in an appreciative or loving way is natural for everyone, no matter what gender they are looking at. Sol wants us to have love in our world, so I don't see why we should limit it."

Andrea widened her eyes, and then she burst

into tears. Sonja hugged her, and stroked her back. "There, there, my child, it's ok."

Sonja hugged the child for some time, feeling both sadness and joy. She was sad because she wished her mother could have been like her in this moment, accepting who she was and seeing the good in the love she had for others, but joy because she was able to be the person this girl needed in this moment.

Andrea sniffed and broke away. She wiped her eyes, and looked at Sonja with awe again. "Thank you so much, Keeper. I know I want to follow you with all my heart now. I was a little lost before, not knowing if my place was here, but now I know if you are here then I should be as well."

She patted Andrea on the shoulder again. "I'm glad." She stood up, and smiled at the girl. "You know, I think I have a job for you."

"Anything, Keeper."

"I'm looking for people that can be my assistants. I definitely feel you could be one of them, but I think I need a few more. If you have any close friends amongst the acolytes that you know do good work, I would love you to bring them to my wagon."

Andrea cried out in excitement. She bowed to

Sonja again, and ran towards the Acolyte's wagon. Sonja watched her go, feeling like she did something important and wondrous. It was one child, but change sometimes started with only one. She could now say to herself that she made someone that was like her feel welcome in the faith and unashamed about who they were. Maybe if that spread to others, another child could feel the same thing, and then maybe all the children would eventually feel it. This shift in thinking could change the teachers' opinions. And when those children became Priests and Priestesses they would teach others the same lesson. Sonja lost herself in that future world where people like her were accepted, which seemed a better of a paradise than even Sol's garden.

But she was jolted out of her dream by the sound of Britta's voice behind her. She turned to the curly haired Head Teacher, sighing. She wondered whether people like Britta would ever accept the vision she had. Not that she could judge Britta at the moment, maybe she just needed the right argument or nudge to see things the way Sonja saw them.

"We need to speak about your new path," Britta said.

"I know," Sonja said. She glanced around at the other faces around Britta, all as hard nosed and furious. "Why don't we conduct this in my wagon?"

The two women sat at the Keeper's desk. Sonja had asked for it to be a personal meeting between the two of them, and Britta assured the others in her group that she could speak for them all. The desk had been cleared of some of the scrolls, but there were still a few out and they weren't placed on the desk neatly. Britta looked down at this with a withering stare.

Sonja sat underneath the Sol Shard. She could feel its warm heat on the back of her neck. She wondered whether Britta held in her hands whether she could be shown the vision of the united caravan. Surely seeing that vision would dispense the need for any argument. But unfortunately not everyone who held the Sol Shard saw a vision, so she would have to try to convince Britta that her way was best the hard way.

"So, my friend and Head Teacher, what is your issue with the path I have set forth for the faith?"

"Do I really need to answer that?" Britta said,

disdain on her face. "You are literally telling people it is ok to do shadow filled things."

"Come now Britta, you have read the scrolls as I have, in fact you have studied them more than I, so you know that what is considered shadow changes with the text and the times. I'm sure you know that in the Scroll of Shadow it talks about how it was once a shadow to have husbands and wives because Aileas' wanted to maximize the amount of children the tribe would produce. We definitely don't consider that a shadow now."

"Yes I agree not all shadows are equal and that we can cull some. But the ones you have suggested we cull are ones we know time and time again cause us trouble. For example, drink leads to overconfidence, violence, and casual sex. All of these are a danger if you want to bring together a community."

"And yet because the wagon train has these parties they have become closer. With their parties they created the Jarl position and a way for that Jarl to get to know what the people want."

Britta shook her head and put her finger down on the desk. "You see you're not thinking about the bigger picture here. Our Mission is to bring people together, and we do that by giving them a goal, a pursuit. That pursuit is one of purity. We need to act better than the average person because it will show how great we are to Sol."

"I agree, our Mission is to bring people together, but we don't do that by pursuing purity. That has alienated us from the others. How many times did our mother have to bring down small rebellions from the workers because they wanted to usurp her? How she could not see those rebellions came about because of her rhetoric I do not know."

At the mention of her mother, Britta scowled. Sonja was surprised by this. She had always felt Britta had a close relationship with their mother, definitely closer than the one she had with her. And then she understood why, and what Britta was really here about.

"You feel our mother made a mistake in making me Keeper," she said.

Britta banged her fist on her table. "Of course I do. I don't get it, I was her assistant all those years. You weren't in the picture in the last decade. I sorted everything out for her, I talked with her, gave her guidance, and yet she picks you."

Sonja sat back, shaking her head. "To be

honest I do not get why I am Keeper either. I did not expect it nor did I really want it. And I'm sure if she saw the path I'm taking now our mother would surely pick a different person."

"Then why are you still in the job?" Britta asked.

"Do you remember when we were proselytizing around Eik? We used to talk to the farmers that had holes in their tunics and smelt like they hadn't bathed in weeks. We walked around the streets, chatting to the homeless artists, and sometimes we would even go into the prisons and pray with them. Do you remember how the Queen and the nobles laughed at us, and only gave us permission to do it because they thought it was a joke? Well, what happened a decade later? All those farmers, artists, and prisoners, built themselves a church to Sol. They gathered together and used their new found faith to bring themselves power. They questioned the rule of the Queen and told everyone that people should question it as well. That is why I'm Keeper. I feel a sense that our Mission can change things for the good, bring people together, and take away the corrupt power that sometimes rules over others. If we do that we get closer to Sol's paradise."

"That's a lovely dream," Britta said, looking down at the table sadly. "But you have to understand what binds people together. People like being together, but they also like being separate. They like the feeling of being special, that by dedicating yourself to the purer path you can feel that you are higher up in the sky and closer to Sol. Our mother saw that."

Sonja was horrified by Britta's message. It said that the only thing that could bring people together was the sense that they were better than others. "Do you now see that philosophy can only divide people?"

"It may do, and yet those people who follow the path will enjoy Sol's paradise. I'll ask you this, do you really want to live in a paradise full of people that do not follow a pure life? That will get violent every time there is a drink, that will have sex with your husband just because they feel like it, that will steal your things and lord over you. If paradise includes everybody, then it will include the nasty people."

"I don't know how you think this," Sonja said, looking at Britta with shock. "But you have a warped sense of what people are like. They are much better than you think. Sure some of them can be violent and want power, but most just want to live their lives in peace and quiet, and work together as a community. I feel the faith can provide that."

Britta looked at her confused. "I don't know how someone that lived in a similar way to me can't see people for the way they are. How many adults in your workhouse just blankly stared at the pain the children were in when they were on the wheel, had no emotion when they dragged the next dead body out of the door?"

"We are not in the workhouse anymore. The people of the wagon train are not like that," she said.

Britta shook her head, and pushed herself up from the desk. "Everyone can be like that. The only way to stop it is to find yourself in a place that rejects those things, and makes you into a better person."

Sonja sighed. "It looks like I'm not going to convince you."

"No you're not."

"Unfortunately you haven't convinced me either. My new path will go ahead."

Britta had a hard look in her eyes. "I thought as much, but you should know this. I will make sure to stop you at every turn. I will protest every action you take, and I will convince others how your plan will ruin the faith."

At that Britta turned, and exited the wagon. Sonja sat at the chair, feeling her heart grow heavy. She didn't feel angry at Britta, more sad. Britta and her shared a similar experience but Britta had learnt a different lesson from it. Sonja had been saved from the darkness by a bright light, and when she looked back at the darkness she could see the light could banish it away. Britta saw the darkness as immovable, and she wanted to carve an area of light it could not penetrate, leaving those within the darkness to their fate. Sonja understood why Britta would feel that staying in the light and not trying to beat the darkness was more comforting, but Sonja saw this went against their morals of saving people. Britta's path would definitely not bring Sol back into the sky.

For a brief second Sonja felt she should fire Britta from the role of Head Teacher. Britta having that leadership role would imbue her protest with more potency. She would be more likely to be heard by the faithful, and some Priests and Priestesses were more likely to follow her. Not to mention the fact that Britta controlled what the

Acolytes were taught, and the conversation showed that Britta would never change those teachings under any circumstance.

But Sonja dismissed the thought of firing. It would look petty, and like she was playing politics. No one knew whether her new path could work, whether they could bring the farmers over to their faith again. If she fired Britta it might just amplify her voice even more. No, the only way to go against Britta was to make sure this harvest festival was the best festival the wagon train ever had.

YOU LOOK BACK AT EVERY SHADOW EXPECTING THE GLINT OF A KNIFE

'The Unhappy King' by Lysanne Lungbourg

Manang ascended into the purplish-blue sky. Its evil red eye pierced Sigrun's. She raised her hands to shield her eyes. She rushed down the streets, trying to get away from Hannes and his army. She didn't care where she was going, the only thing she cared about was trying to understand what she just saw and what it meant.

Hannes was training an army to attack the faith, probably in the hopes of claiming power for himself and the workers of the wagon train. Gregor and Yael must have known about this, which was why they voted him out as Jarl. However instead of saying that, the Elders had used the empty food stores as the excuse to vote him out.

But why did they need that excuse? Why hide what Hannes was doing? Surely building an army against the faith would have been a better excuse to be voted out than the food thing? And why didn't they tell her about this? She was Jarl and this was an important danger to her and the wagon train. What were Gregor and Yael really planning?

She didn't know, and it hurt her head to think about the different ways the two Elders had played politics with this. Again, she felt she was a piece on a *King's Game* board. The people playing had an idea of what move they were making with her piece, but she had no clue whether she was meant for a maneuver, or a sacrifice.

Should she confront Yael and Gregor, ask them why they had voted Hannes out but kept any mention of his activities secret? What would they do if she told them she knew their secret? Would they vote her out, put in place one of their lackeys, or was this the kind of knowledge that they would kill to keep secret?

When Sigrun stumbled into her wagon, she placed one of the armchairs in front of the door. She might have been exaggerating the danger, but in that moment she feared either Hannes', Gregor's, or Yael's men bashing in the door. She just needed time to think and calm down.

She took the second posh whiskey bottle from the desk drawer, poured a glass, and sat down in the armchair. What should she do?

She drank the glug of whiskey and poured

another shot straight after. Was this really what being a Jarl was? Would she always have to look at everyone with suspicion? Would they always have dark motives that would go against hers? Would she always have to be wary of any knife the important family members were holding just in case they backstabbed her? If that was the case why was she doing the job? The only danger from herding cows had been a potential stampede, other than that it was a slow and boring job. She didn't have to worry about others manipulating or wanting to kill her. Why couldn't she go back to that?

Could she go back to that? Could she just say to Yael and Gregor that the job wasn't for her and she wanted to go back to the old one. Would they get suspicious?

She downed the shot of whiskey. The strong smoky taste overwhelmed her and made her neck twinge.

Sigrun dismissed the idea of giving up on the title. She did actually believe the thing she told Yael and Gregor that night, how the people needed a new goal to pursue. Whether she was the right person to enact that, she was unsure, but she felt she should give it a go. She had been miserable as a cattle rancher and had wanted to get this job. Also she probably was the only other who knew about Hannes' army and could stop it, apart from the Elders. But they had tried to hide that fact, so she was unsure whether they wanted to stop it.

Even though she wasn't at all religious, she didn't want Hannes to attack the faith. She imagined his army rushing at the yellow robed Priests and Priestesses. Sonja at the front being slashed by swords, blood leaking out on the grass below. Hannes smiling as he stepped onto the Keeper's podium, smashing it to bits.

How could she stop Hannes? Now her oven idea felt way too slow. They would have to wait a few days for the harvest festival to end, and then it would take about a week to get to Munn. They would then have to bargain for the ovens, and convince the Mattsons that she was prepared to give them to workers. Her and the Mattsons would then have to sit down and strike a deal. In all this time Hannes would be building and training his army. If he saw the oven thing was a big threat, he would probably strike against the faith early. It wasn't certain whether Hannes would win against the faith, but even if he lost he would still kill many faithful, maybe even Sonja.

So what was a faster way to get rid of him? She could get a vote to remove the Administrator from his post, and to try and install one she could trust. But that would piss Hannes and the Mattsons off. The two of them would make sure her life and the lives of Baldurs and Hoademakers would be as horrible as possible. Plus she would need Yael and Gregor on board, and they might be suspicious of why the vote was happening, or not want to vote because of the problems it would cause them.

Was there a way to limit the parties or the amount of food the parties used? Because that was what Hannes used as his main recruitment method. If she could prevent the weekly parties she could slow down Hannes.

Yes, that seemed like a sensible path. She would have to get votes for it, but she felt that could be feasible. The point about preventing the overuse of food would be attractive to Gregor, and it would mean she could stop Hannes without Gregor getting suspicious that she knew about the army. She also felt that she could easily get Sonja's and the faith to vote for it. They had always wanted to moderate the parties, and she could sell this to them as a way to make sure parties were about getting together as a community instead of being hedonistic. She probably would have to experience some wrath from the Mattsons about it, but she felt she could handle that for the period of time it took to truly get rid of Hannes.

Sigrun smiled as she drank the last glug of whiskey. She screwed the top of the bottle closed, stood up, and pulled the chair away from the door. If Yael and Gregor wanted to do politics, she was fine with that, she would just outplay them in the field.

QUEEN VERA'S VIOLENT DISPOSAL WAS DUE TO THE UNPOPULARITY OF HER MEAT TAX

'The Book of Disastrous Kings & Queens' by Isabella Dahlman

Sonja stepped into the storage wagon. The air felt cool and dry. There was an earthy smell from all the vegetables, which made her think of Sigrun for the thousandth time. On both sides of the square wagon were boxes filled with carrots, cucumbers, leaks, radishes, lettuce, and all manner of other veg. Built into the top of the wagon was a large compartment filled with wheat, grain, and oats. The faithful had everything they needed to make a great feast, if you loved salads and bread. But Sonja knew that the farmers would want good meat, and they had none of it.

"We haven't had meat in years," the Quartermaster, Sigmund, said, as he showed Sonja around the storage wagon. "Not since the Mattsons took a dislike to us."

"Wasn't that when Hannes came on board?" she asked, remembering a vague memory of her mother talking with Rita Mattson and a thin man with brushed back blond hair. "I remember the argument not going well between the two of them."

"A few days afterwards the Keeper put her first purification law in, saying consuming meat was a shadow," Sigmund said, checking a few of the boxes of vegetables.

Sonja shook her head. It felt like such an obvious move to ban the consumption of meat when they couldn't eat it anymore. Instead of looking like a set back it looked like a moral choice. She couldn't believe anyone fell for it, but then again at the time she had fallen for it, probably because no one knew the real reason behind the move. Her mother never shared, she was very clever like that.

"Well we won't have a successful harvest festival without meat," she said.

"You would have to go to the Mattsons for that I'm afraid," Sigmund said, grimacing.

Sonja also grimaced, and sighed. "Surely they will see this isn't just for us but for the wagon train as well."

"You'd hope so, but I'll warn you there is word that the Mattsons don't like the Baldurs either now. And they're going to be the ones mostly coming to this harvest festival."

"Well healing divisions starts today," she said,

not totally feeling the inspiration behind her own words. But as ever all she could do was try.

The Mattsons, plus their cooks and butchers, had pitched themselves on the west side of the wagon train. They had subtly moved their wagons away from the rest, meaning there was more grass to walk across to get to their little enclave. A declaration to anyone who saw it that they had issues with the rest of the caravan.

As Sonja walked down Rod street she felt a chill in the air. The red haired and freckled faces, standing on their wagon's front axle or sitting on chairs at the side of the street, watched her with icy eyes. Many frowned or spat on the ground when she walked past. When one Mattson saw her, he widened his eyes and ran down the street.

When she got into Mattson square there was now a crowd gathered to watch her. Though unlike the faithful or even the farmer's crowd, this group of men and women had hard faces and narrowed eyed stares. Many mumbled to their neighbors, but a few shouted at her to fuck off and get back to her encampment.

She felt a little intimidated. Men and women stepped up to her, shaking their fists. Thankfully she had brought a sword, and gripped it whenever anyone got too close.

She pushed her way to the wagon in the middle of the square. It was painted with bright red and gold colors, with the Mattson runes swirled on the wood. It stood on gleaming silver axles and wheels. Standing at the front, watching her coolly, was Rita Mattson.

Rita was a stick figure of a woman, with a grandma bob to her hair that had gone gray. But her weathered face and hard stare was surprisingly intimidating. It was known that any Mattson that got a point from her finger or a raised voice had to do everything in their power to apologize, otherwise they were going to clean up blood in Slakter Row for the rest of their lives. Sonja wondered whether she could convince a woman like that, and what she would have to give to do so.

She nodded to Rita. "I'm just here to talk. It's only me. Can you call off your family?"

Rita waved her hand at the crowd, who all gave Sonja one last narrowed eyed look and dispersed amongst the Square and the streets.

Sonja breathed out, and took her hand off the sword. "Thank you."

"What is it you want to talk about, Keeper?"

Rita said the last word with as much hatred and bitterness as she could muster.

"I wondered whether I could get some meat for the harvest festival."

Rita jumped down from her wagon. "What's the deal with that? Are you trying to lure the farmers in so you can surround them with your faithful and get them to convert to Sol by the sword."

"Nothing of the sort, I'm trying to build bridges between us and the wagon train."

Rita laughed. "You failed with that as soon as you became high and mighty, saying that the things that we found fun in this ice cold world were shadows that should be stamped out."

Sonja bowed her head, looking to the grass below. "We were wrong to do that. I hope to make amends."

Rita furrowed her brow. "I don't believe it."

"You can come to the harvest festival yourself if you want. If you see it for yourself you might believe it."

"Nah, I'm good. You're not getting your meat."

Sonja looked up in annoyance. "Just like that. It's not just the faithful you are hurting, you know, it's the people. I know you dislike the leaders but I don't think you want to piss the ordinary people off. They are Hannes biggest supporters."

"You're right, I don't want to piss off Hannes' biggest supporters," Rita said, grinning. "But it's not me pissing them off, it's you. If you don't supply meat they'll just think it's the typical faith crap of making them follow your rules, and they'll never accept you."

"Why do you hate us?" Sonja said, feeling sad that someone else could have such destructive views about a group of people.

"Did you know that Hannes and my great grandmother came from the same place? And what's even funnier is they both ran away for the same reason. Because the town of Tro was run by people like you, faithful. They prayed to Sol all the time and followed their bloody codes, but if you didn't, if you wanted to have fun or be different, they punished you severely. Yes, it is ironic that my great grandmother and Hannes ran away to a faithful wagon train, but at the time your power was waning and they saw an opportunity. I'm just seizing my own opportunity."

Rita smiled again and climbed back onto the wagon. Sonja wanted to say more, how she was nothing like the faith in the town nor was she like her mother anymore. But it looked like Rita wasn't prepared to listen/ She waved Sonja off.

The crowd emerged from their wagons again, ready to intimidate her. Once again, she put her hand back on her sword hilt and pushed through a crowd full of hard faces. She walked out of Mattsons' Square feeling angry and disappointed.

She hadn't gotten her meat, and it felt like her goal of uniting the wagon train would hit a block when it came to the Mattsons.

GETTING VOTES THROUGH THE COUNCIL IS ALL ABOUT WINING, DINING, AND MAKING TRADES

'Diary of Jarl Jeanette Arnoldson'

Ever since being revealed to be the Jarl, Sigrun found herself in more and more uneasy interactions with the people of the wagon train. When she joined a group of farmers on their lunch break, the farmers would stare at her fine cloak and brooch with mistrust. The conversation the farmers were having would change to one of mundane matters, or would stop altogether. She tried to use her easy charm and joking manner to get them talking again, but most were not convinced. After a day of constant frustration she asked one group why they were being so cagey, and they told her that she was the Jarl and so they had to be wary of what they said to her. Protesting by saying she would not use their words against them only went on deaf ears.

Her interactions with the important Baldurs weren't that much better. Sven Baldur always had time for her, trying to make her feel welcome in the group. But it didn't seem to ingratiate herself with the other men and women in fine cloaks. They always looked at her with disdain, like they were looking at some horse shit on their shoe. Even when she managed to instigate a conversation they would speak slowly to her, and assumed she couldn't possibly know anything of value.

Sigrun couldn't understand this shift. In parties she used to be able to talk to both commoners and important people alike. Everyone seemed to love her attitude and her jokes. But now that she was Jarl she was drifting more and more away from the people she was supposed to help. How would she know what actions to take if they wouldn't talk with her, how would she get the important family members on board if they looked down on her?

Another question came to her: how was Hannes loved by the people? Because it felt to her, from what farmers and important Baldurs had said, that they both got on with him and even liked him. Whenever they thought she was not around - and sometimes when she was around - the people talked about how they missed Hannes and how he had a better personality. What had Hannes done so differently?

It was a mystery but one that she would have to work out later, as she had more important Hannes business to deal with. She had to stop his army recruiting, and to do that she had to get a vote from Gregor Baldur in the council for her law reducing parties.

The farmers in Bonde Square were hard at work, scything stalks of wheat, corn, or oats, examining bushes for ripened veg and fruit, or bent over pulling out bushels of carrots or potatoes. The day's temperature was warm, the world had transitioned into spring. All the farmers had sweaty brows and tired looks.

She walked past the farmers, feeling their narrowed eyed gaze. Her new cloak and tunic felt itchy and uncomfortable in the heat, and the brooch kept on banging against her chest. As Jarl nothing felt right anymore: her confident walk had been replaced by a heavy plod, her easy going smile had turned into a frown, and her loving audience had turned into a suspicious clique.

Gregor Baldur's wagon was as long and wide as two wagons, looking like a town home on wheels. Painted on the side were large white runes, within dark yellow and brown swirls. Jutting out of the wagon was a small veranda, which sat a table and chairs. Sitting on one of these chairs, absorbed in her sewing, was Gregor's wife Joan.

Joan had a hawk-like face and piercing eyes. Sigrun didn't announce herself, boldly ascending the veranda stairs. She knocked on the table.

Joan looked up at her, but didn't seem surprised. "I'm afraid my husband is indisposed at the moment, feeling sick it seems."

Sigrun had heard rumors that Gregor had not been seen outside for a while. When Sven wasn't in the group of family members, they talked about how Gregor might have a serious sickness, and he might not even have long to live. As with most rumors, Sigrun took them with a grain of salt.

"I can still speak to you, you have as much power and influence on things as your husband does, even though he does all the voting," she said, sitting down opposite Joan.

Joan put down her thread on the table. "I guess I've persuaded him to vote on a few laws. So what do I owe the pleasure of the Jarl's presence?"

Sigrun put up her hand. "Please, we are equals here."

"I know, but you learn to emphasize the importance of people in leadership roles in this place. I find that many leaders just like to feel they are on a pedestal. Hannes definitely loved me saying how great he was and how I was so grateful to be in his presence."

"I bet he did. But I'm not like that. I come from a muddy background and to be honest I feel uncomfortable in my fancy tunic. It feels itchy around the neck."

Joan leaned forwards, and whispered. "My advice is if it doesn't suit you, take it off and go back to your old clothes. Or you will have to lean more into power and prestige, make everyone recognize that you're better than them." She gestured to the veranda. "Gregor can lean into the grandeur of power, in fact people expect it of him. The worst option is to go half way, people on the lower end will hate you because you act like an important person, but the important people will hate you because you act uncouth and like you are below them."

That seemed to hit the nail into the horseshoe for what was happening to her. Maybe the way she acted when she was a cattle rancher had a power to it. Her muddy look and drunken attitude showed to everyone that she didn't care, and that disarmed people and made them comfortable to talk to her. And when they found out that she was actually intelligent and had good ideas it surprised them enough that it made them remember her.

Sigrun felt the fine texture of the tunic and the raised runes of her brooch. Did she have to rethink how she was going about as Jarl? Did she have to really look the part?

"Anyway I'm guessing you didn't come here to get leadership advice," Joan said, sitting up straight in her chair. "What did you want to talk to me about?"

"I won't deny it's very nice to get advice," she said, nodding her thanks for it. "But you are right I'm here for another reason. I'm going to enact a law that limits the amount of parties that the wagon train will be able to throw. It will also stipulate the amount of food and drink that can be used within those parties, and ban the use of food for other parties. I was wondering whether I could get Gregor's vote for that."

Joan looked surprised. "You are going to limit parties?"

"I know the irony, the person known for enjoying parties is going to limit them. But it's precisely because I've been to them, know how much waste they create, know how chaotically they are planned, that makes me understand that they need to be more...uniform."

"Where's this really coming from?"

Sigrun took a sharp intake of breath. She appreciated how Joan saw right through her plan, and knew that something lay behind this law beyond her excuse. It was a lesson that Sigrun herself was having to get better at: seeing the true reason behind others' actions.

Unfortunately, she couldn't let Joan know the true reason behind her law. She still didn't know why Gregor had hidden the fact Hannes had been building up an army, and she didn't know what he would do if he found out she knew.

"Your husband's passion about the misuse of food and how we nearly starved to death has really gotten to me," she said.

Joan gave her a narrowed eye look. It had been a lame response, and she suspected Joan knew it was bullshit, but at least Joan didn't know why and that was important.

"The issue is the people," Joan said, picking up her thread from the table. "Gregor knows that people love the parties, and hates the past attempts by the faith to get rid of them. So I feel it would be tricky for him to vote on a law like this, something that looks like it comes from the faith.

He's already in the shit with his workers over voting off Hannes with the faith."

"So that means he wouldn't vote for this?" Sigrun said, a little deflated.

"Not necessarily, he just has to know whether the people will be on board with it."

"Of course they aren't going to be on board with it, even if it's sensible to do so. As soon as you take something away from people, they are going to be unhappy and demand it back. You see it in children."

Joan clicked her sewing needles together. "Yes, but as a mother I know ways to convince children on why it's best to not have the thing they want, or to bribe them with some other thing they want more. I would guess the same could be done with people."

Damn, Joan was good! "Ah, so you are saying I should convince the wagon train to go with this plan."

"I will tell you I've been impressed by your ability to do this Jarl job," Joan said, giving her a withering glance. "But you are sometimes awfully slow on the uptake."

ONE LOVER SAYS THAT'S A FINE RIVER BOAT

'Two Lovers Meet' Skald Song

The Keepers wagon was always too bright to sleep in. Where the Keeper actually slept was through a door on the side of the wall, which led to a small square room with a double bed and a wardrobe. When shut, the door looked like it was one with the wooden wall. The bedroom was where Sonja went when she didn't want to be disturbed.

Sonja sat on the bed, shoulders slumped. She stared at the jug placed on the bedside table, which held the redhead girl's gift of a rose. She liked staring at it when she got into bed. It gave her hope that the two sides of the wagon train could be united. But at the moment she stared at its green stem and small thorns.

She hated that Rita would willingly sabotage the harvest festival just to make sure the faithful looked bad. It made Sonja question whether there could ever be unity in the wagon train, when there were elements like Rita who wanted to get rid of one side. Though she had to admit Rita wasn't alone in that, there was also Britta on her side that wanted to get rid of the non-faithful.

How could she go against these sides that would never move no matter how much you told them what they were doing damaged the people they said they cared about?

Her first thought was to try to get rid of these elements, but she understood straight away that would be just as bad. It would just show others that the faith was intolerant and wanted control. But it would also just be doing the same thing Rita and Britta advocated. Instead of learning to live with your opponents and sometimes having to listen to what they had to say, you just purged them and made sure the rest of your group agreed. Having read the scrolls and learnt what happened to Aileas and the creation of the Mission, she understood that even that would never solve anything for long. Thinking always changed throughout the years, and a group of like minded individuals eventually turned into ones who had different ideas to one another.

Sonja sighed. She couldn't really focus on that grander question of how to unify the wagon train. How to do it just made her feel overwhelmed and like she was too small for the job. All she could do was focus on what she needed to do now, which was get meat for the party. If she could do that she could go against Rita's wishes, and bring the wagon train closer together, even just a little.

But how could she get meat? She couldn't get any butchers to secretly give her any, they were all under the Mattsons' control. She would have to find someone else to cut up the meat. Could some cattle ranchers do that? They knew how to look after cows and sheep, did that mean some of them knew how to kill and butcher them. The two seemed very separate now but there had been a time, when the wagon train was smaller than it was now, where the two jobs were the same. Were there any of the old cattle ranchers that had passed butchering skills down through their family?

There was only one person she knew that could give her that answer, Sigrun. Thinking about Sigrun warmed her heart and made her a little excited.

She carefully took the rose out of the jug and put it in her pocket. It had been too long since they saw each other, so she felt it would be a good present to give to Sigrun.

Sonja strode out of the faith encampment, going towards the Jarl's wagon. By sheer coincidence Sigrun was striding towards the faith encampment. They glanced each other's way, surprised but delighted.

"I was just coming to talk to you about something," Sigrun said, laughing.

"What a stroke of luck, I was coming to you to talk as well," Sonja said, her heart pounding.

"Should we go to my wagon or yours?"

"Yours seems closer."

Sonja looked around but couldn't see any onlookers. There would have definitely been a crowd if they walked into the encampment.

"Should I get my whiskey bottle out?" Sigrun asked, staring at her with flirtatious eyes. There definitely was a spark of energy between the two of them.

"I think a meeting is always enhanced by some alcohol," Sonja said, grinning.

Sigrun laughed and gestured for them to go to the wagon. They walked as close as they could get away with, each glancing back at the other, smiling and laughing as they did. It felt like they both communicated the same thing to each other, words of longing and desire. Even though it was a short walk, it felt like an eternity to Sonja. She just wanted to touch Sigrun then and there.

Sonja slammed the door as soon as she got in. There wasn't time for a hello, or really anytime for a breath. They just kissed like no one was watching. Sonja grabbed Sigrun's back and kissed down her neck. When she got to the shoulder blade, Sigrun's breath quickened. Sonja was about to dive down further, when Sigrun shook her head and pushed her away.

Their faces were red, and Sonja felt a little light headed. She looked at Sigrun confused. "Don't you want this?"

"More than anything, but we both wanted to see each other for a reason."

The thought about meat and cattle ranchers had completely gone from Sonja's mind. She stepped back, feeling a little embarrassed about how swept up she had been. Surely as a sensible leader she could push away her desires for one second and do what she came here to do.

Sigrun shook her head, walked to the desk, and poured two glasses of whiskey. She handed one of them to Sonja and sat down in the armchair. Sonja sat down in the armchair opposite, a desk and embarrassment in the way of the two of them now. They drank their whiskeys in an awkward silence, glancing towards one another.

Sigrun laughed. "We are just like a couple of teenagers that have just been caught by our mums. What did you come to me to talk about."

Sonja's head throbbed, but she breathed in to calm herself and think about what she originally came here for. "I just wanted to know whether there were any cattle ranchers you knew that could butcher their own meat. The Mattsons are refusing to give us any and we do need some if we are going to make this harvest festival a success."

"You know weirdly enough my thing was connected to the Mattsons as well," Sigrun said, raising her eyebrows.

"It's almost like Sol wanted us to come together."

Sonja flashed to the vision she saw of her and Sigrun in white dresses kissing one another and uniting the wagon train. She drank her whiskey, feeling the joy and hope of that moment. Maybe this was the start of it.

"Well I'm glad Sol wanted us to come together. I wanted to ask whether you would vote for a law that will limit the amount of parties," Sigrun said.

Sonja looked at her in surprise. "That seems a strange law for a caravaner to suggest."

"Yeah I guess you can say my partying phase is over," Sigrun said, staring into her whiskey. "But really it's to try to take away the parties Hannes and the Mattsons are running. Look I can tell you something and it won't go out of this wagon, right?"

"You think I'm going to say anything about a secret tryst between two lovers of the same gender to my lot?" Sonja said, laughing.

"Good point. Well, I found out the other night that Hannes was using the weekly parties to recruit people for his own army. And do you know who that army has its sights on: the faithful."

Sonja shifted in her armchair. "You're saying Hannes, and the Mattsons who ally with him, want to attack us?"

Sigrun nodded.

The two of them took big swigs from their drink. Sonja felt a little chill in the air. So Rita wasn't just willing to make sure her party was a disaster, she was also willing to kill her and the faithful to get what she wanted.

"Can't this be stopped?" she asked.

"That's what I'm trying to do with this partying law. If I can limit the parties then I can take away some of Hannes' recruitment. That will give us time to get the people on our side. Once they are, we can get rid of Hannes for good."

"Why can't we get rid of him now?"

"Unfortunately the people quite like him. probably because of the whole going against a faith that wants to force purity on others thing, mainly," Sigrun said, grimacing.

"It's ok, I didn't like it much either."

They both laughed at that, and finished their glasses of whiskey. Sigrun poured more.

"What you say about Hannes and the rest disturbs me, so we should probably try bringing in this law to see if it stops anything. I think I can get three of my faithful to vote with you, that'll make five overall."

Sigrun furrowed her brow. "What happens when there is a deadlock in the Council?"

"I've never been on it so I don't know, and I don't remember my mother saying it ever happened."

Sigrun drank a glug of whiskey, and waved her hand. "Well I'm hoping to get the farmers on board with the law anyway so that'll get me Gregor."

The two of them sat and drank their whiskey. They were finished with business but the seriousness of the conversation and the embarrassment from earlier had sucked any excitement and passion from the air between them. The two glanced at each other. Sonja wanted to go to Sigrun and kiss her, but the desk was in the way.

"I'm sorry, I kind of killed the mood didn't I?" Sigrun said.

"I guess it's something we have to get used to, being leaders and all. Not every meeting we have can be...kissing."

"Nothing would get done if that was the case," Sigrun said, tittering.

Sonja laughed. "We need to organize a time when we can see each other and not talk about politics."

"I agree, what about after the harvest festival? When people are drunk and you can relax because you have done your job"

"That just seems a long way away," Sonja said, sighing. It was only a few days but now that they had that passionate kiss today she wanted it to be that night.

"I know, but we still have the problem of being seen. I tried to sneak into your encampment and was nearly caught by the guard."

"You did?" Sonja laughed, feeling a little warmth that Sigrun would risk herself to see her.

Sigrun nodded. "Yeah, not one of my finest

ideas."

They both drank the last of their whiskeys. Sigrun slapped the felt green of the desk. "Well best get you to meet those cattle ranchers."

The two of them got up from their chairs. Sonja strode towards the door, but then remembered what was in her pocket.

She carefully took out the rose. "I got you something."

Sigrun looked to the rose, then to her. Her eyes widened and she put her hand on her breast.

Sigrun wrapped her hands around Sonja's waist, and kissed her. The kiss grew urgent, and both grabbed at clothes and took them off. Sonja kissed down Sigrun's neck again, joyful that she was able to touch her like this. Sigrun moaned.

Sonja pushed her on the armchair. In that moment she didn't care about politics, meat, or whether she could unify the wagon train. She just delved into showing the passion and joy she felt towards Sigrun.

> DO NO FRET IF YOU LOSE YOUR WAY. THERE IS
> ALWAYS A PART OF YOU THAT KNOWS YOUR
> TRUE SELF. LISTEN TO IT AND YOU'LL
> REDISCOVER THE RIGHT PATH
>
> *'Meditations' by Wilbur Paige*

Sigrun had never had sex like *that* before. There had been an overwhelming sense of joy and pleasure. Her heart had beat like a drum and her brain exploded when she had climaxed. Her whole body had been left shaken for a few minutes. She had loved sex with other partners, but there was something about the relationship she had with Sonja that had made this time more special. This hadn't been a moment of fun, it was more spiritual than that, like she had been communing with Sol. She wondered whether she should say as much to Sonja, but worried that might be blasphemous.

The two of them never made it to the bed. They laid on the wooden floor, cuddling up to one another. Sigrun was uncomfortable and comfortable, uncomfortable because the floor was hard and cold, comfortable because it felt so warm and right to have her arm around Sonja's body.

Sonja stirred. Sigrun kissed down her neck. Sonja groaned in pleasure, but slowly moved her head away.

"I have to do what I came here to do," Sonja said, disappointment on her face.

"You didn't come here to do that?" Sigrun said, grinning.

"Unfortunately not. But I will say that it was definitely better than the times I paid for it."

"Oh, about that...didn't I tell you I was going to charge?"

They both laughed and slowly pushed themselves up, picking up their clothes off the floor. While they were dressing, Sigrun stared at Sonja's naked body, appreciating her curves, her thick arms, her narrow face, and her long black hair. She wanted to remember that body in her mind before it got covered up by clothes. She didn't feel she was going to see it all that often.

The cool breeze outside was a nice balm to the heat in the wagon. Manang's red eye slowly moved in and out of white clouds, every time it popped out a ray of reddish light cast down onto the ground.

Both Sigrun and Sonja walked a little apart from each other, trying to act normal to the few people that were around the Jarl's wagon. They both occasionally glanced towards the other, trying to stifle laughs. It felt like they were naughty children trying to hide a big secret.

Sigrun was too far away from Sonja. She wanted to be right next to her, holding her hand. She wanted to tell everyone in the wagon train that they were together and they could screw themselves if they had a problem with it. But she knew that it would jeopardize Sonja's leadership.

It felt weird to have that power over someone else. With one move – whether she would willingly do it or accidentally do it – she could bring down the leadership of the faith. Some Jarls, like Hannes, would have loved to have that power. But she felt uncomfortable with it. The two of them were leaders, which meant that they would probably have political disagreements. She didn't want Sonja to think that she would use that power to gain an advantage, it would break them apart and the pieces would never fit back together again.

They entered Kveg Plain in silence. Sigrun and Sonja kept glancing at each other, their eyes saying they wished they could be close to one another. Sigrun felt a weight in her heart. The joy she felt being with Sonja was now mixed with a sadness that they couldn't be together totally. She had no choice but to focus on what she came here to do.

Sigrun scanned the plain of grass, hearing cows and sheep in the distance. The air smelled like a mixture of fresh air and animal dung, which made her feel at home. If Sonja wasn't there she would have walked across the plain, looking out into the world beyond and imagining herself exploring it. She wondered whether her wagon was still there and whether anyone had moved in, but realized she should be wondering who to talk to about getting meat for the festival.

There were three cattle ranchers that could butcher their own meat. The friendliest to her would be Edven. On the occasional evening, when the sky was clear, she would go over to his wagon with a chair and they would drink whiskey while looking above at the twinkling stars. It had been Edven that taught her that some of the brighter, rounder stars actually moved across the sky, and could be places that were just like the earth they were sitting on: full of trees, grass, and animals. She remembered being fascinated by this, as it reminded her of the fantastical fables that talked about strange creatures coming from the sky.

Edven lived on the east side of the plain. She led the way, looking around at the grass and the cows, feeling more and more strongly that she wanted to come back here. Occasionally, she glanced back at Sonja who was looking towards the edge of the wagon train. There was a yellow shimmer of the Sol Shard barrier. Neither of them spoke, lost in their own world of thought.

Edven stood amongst a flock of sheep. He rested against a pole, while his dog scampered around the sheep, barking. Edven had a long, weathered face, with a bushy mustache, and the hands that gripped the pole were bony.

"Seen anymore wanderers since I've been gone, Edven," she shouted to him.

Edven jumped a little, almost like he had been asleep. He gave her a questioning stare. "They told me you had become Jarl."

"Huh, I thought it took months for news to come around here. They told you right."

She waded through the sheep, and gave Edven a hug. She noticed that Sonja stood a little at a distance, looking at the sheep with a wary stare.

"Don't worry, they won't stampede with the dog there," she said.

Sonja didn't look comfortable about it, but

waded through the flock of sheep. Edven stared at her flame robes, and bowed deeply. "What do I owe the pleasure of having the Keeper here?"

"I've been told by Sigrun that you can butcher your own meat," Sonja said. Sigrun noticed that her voice had changed slightly when talking to Edven, it had a lighter, more airy quality to it.

Edven gave a worried glance towards Sigrun. She patted his shoulder. "Nothing to worry about Edven, she's not here to blame you for doing shadow filled things. She would just like to get some meat from you."

Sonja looked down at the ground in embarrassment. "Sorry, I should have explained myself better. I'm putting on a harvest festival for the wagon train but we do not have any meat. The Mattsons refuse to give us some, but I've heard you can do some butchering and can get around the Mattsons."

"I thought meat was banned in your faith," Edven said, confused.

"I hope to change that," Sonja said.

"Come on Edven, we don't want people to be disappointed because they can't get their teeth into a good lamb shank. The Keeper here wants to show how the faithful have changed and wants to actually be part of the wagon train."

Sonja gave her an impressed look, which Sigrun felt a little pride from. She wanted to be seen by Sonja as someone that was reliable.

Edven glanced between the two of them. The dog barked, and some sheep called out. He smacked the pole on the ground. "I'll do it if you give me one of those shiny stones you have in your storage."

Sigrun was surprised that Edven was dictating terms to her. She thought she would get him on board because they were friends. "They are for trading with towns."

"Well I'm not someone in a town, but I guess you could call this a trade."

"But aren't we friends?"

Edven gripped the pole, looked up into the sky, and sighed. "Not if you are Jarl. Look at that fancy tunic and cloak, and your brooch with those runes, I have none of that."

"But I'm still the same person that drank whiskey and looked out at the stars with," she said. Edven's words echoed the conversation she had with Joan.

"Do you remember in those evenings how we would grumble about the current Jarl," Edven said, looking at her dead on. "We would talk about how we wished they could speak to us sometimes, give us a chance to tell us where to go, give us a chance to settle in some place and enjoy the warm weather or the good town we were in. But those Jarl's never did. I'm afraid since you're Jarl you'll probably be the same."

"That's not true, I became Jarl so I could do what the people wanted."

Edven shook his head. "There are too many people and they each have different ideas of what they want. I won't blame you for your decision, it'll probably be for the good of the wagon train. But sometimes it won't be good for me. And for that reason I'd like to get something now, while you need me."

Sigrun didn't know what to say. One of the people that she was closest to was saying that they couldn't be close because she was the leader. It felt wrong and unfair. Why did being a leader have to change their friendship?

She shook her head. "You'll get your stone,"

"Thank you," Edven said. He bowed to Sonja.

Sigrun turned around and stomped through the herd of sheep, not caring about the cries of complaint from them. She heard the flap of robes behind her, and felt a hand on her shoulder.

"It's ok," Sonja said.

She glanced behind her. "It's not ok. I don't want to be a leader if it means my friends aren't my friends anymore."

Sonja looked down, looking unsure of what to say. Then she stared at her with loving eyes. "You'll always have me."

That stare and those words brought warmth into her heart. She squeezed Sonja's hand. "But I can't have you the way I want."

And she strode off into the plain, leaving Sonja looking out to her sadly. Part of her wanted to go back and cuddle her, but part of her wanted to be alone now. The latter part won out.

Sigrun wandered back to her old wagon. The shabby arched frame still stood there, though the trailer that held the cows were gone, and there were no longer any horses tied to the front. It looked abandoned and lonely in the middle of the grass.

She went up to its side, feeling the roughness of the wood. It was still warm to the touch, almost inviting her to come in. She opened the door, its creak very familiar. The inside looked the same as it had when she had left: empty.

The wardrobe door was open. She rushed towards it. Inside were all her old, muddy clothes. She shouted in joy. She immediately took off her fine cloak and tunic, and put on her old one. It smelled funny and was covered in mud stains, but it felt much more comfortable to wear than the new one had. She threw the new tunic into the wardrobe, and was about to throw the cloak away but then she saw the brooch.

It was the only thing she had that had her family's runes on it. Could she really chuck it away? But then she felt the metal, and saw it gleaming in the crack of sun from the slats. The brooch looked too valuable. It just didn't fit her.

She put her hand on her braid and felt the knots. Those were her true runes, the thing that connected her to her family. That braid felt more important to keep than the brooch did. She opened the door, and threw the brooch out.

Wearing her old clothes and being in this wagon, she couldn't help but stand up straighter, feel more herself. Joan had been right, she had tried to both be down to earth and above their station and it had not worked. The important Baldurs had avoided her, and the people like the farmers or Edven had mistrusted her. But that would be the case no longer, she would go back to the way she had been before: confident, cocky, and very messy.

She glanced towards the bed. She wished she could sleep in it tonight, that way she would actually feel comfortable again. It was a shame to be in messy and muddy clothes that fit, but have to live in a Jarls wagon that was nice looking but didn't fit.

And then an idea came to her. This wagon was empty and it seemed no one had moved in. Why shouldn't she just live in it again? She would have to find where Gregor and Yael had stored the horses, and then move it to the center of the wagon train, but that didn't seem too difficult.

Yes, that would be what she would do. Forget the majesty and poshness of being Jarl, her leadership would be different. She would reflect the muddy, messy people, and she would live in a shambling, rough wooden wagon.

As she felt the knots of her braid, she could almost see her mother smiling at her decision.

THE BREAK UP OF A FRIENDSHIP IS ALWAYS WORSE THAN BREAKING UP WITH A LOVER. YOUR RIPPING UP A DEEPER BOND, FEELING HURT AND LOST IN THE PROCESS

'The Personal Feelings Of Queen Henrietta'

Sonja wanted to follow Sigrun when she walked off to comfort her, but she understood that Sigrun needed some alone time to think things through. Living with a bunch of girls in the same wagon, you learnt very quickly that when they rushed outside the dormitory wagon that it was better to leave them alone. Everyone knew that if you looked upset or cried in the wagon you were likely to get a gaggle of girls coming over to you to work out what was wrong. Sonja couldn't deny that the few times she did cry in front of others and got girls to come over she liked the attention.

She felt sad that she couldn't help Sigrun, but the best thing to do was to leave her to her thoughts and focus on something else. Someone as confident and sure of herself as Sigrun would eventually work it out, and Sonja would surely see her being bright and cheery again. In the meantime her job was to get the faithful ready for the harvest festival.

When she returned to the faith encampment she was surprised how little had been completed. The field didn't have enough tables, chairs, bonfires, or cooking sections for the amount of people that were coming to the festival.

Sonja scanned the encampment to see what had gone wrong. Yellow robed faithful were running about doing one job, but a person would tell them another job was needed and then they would run towards that instead. A man would haul out a table, abandon it to gather wood, then dump that wood pile in a corner to run into the stores to get some food. She sighed, thinking that surely someone would have tried to order this chaos while she had been away, but she guessed that was going to have to be her job.

She strode through the field. Some faithful quickly bowed to her when she walked past, but thankfully they were too focused on their jobs to want a Sol sign or prayer. She looked for her friends amongst the to and fro of the faithful, and found them near the storage wagon, talking with Sigmund.

She smiled at Roose, Teresa, and Sigmund. All three bowed their heads, but they did not smile back.

"What is wrong, my friends?" she asked.

"Britta is making trouble again," Roose said. "She's gotten every Acolyte in the teaching room and told them that they are not allowed to help with the party."

"Plus the fact that we are not doing so well with getting the party organized," Teresa added.

"Well that was what I came over here to sort out. I think some defined jobs for different groups are needed. Roose I want you to gather the Priests and get them to put the tables and chairs onto the field, Teresa I want you to get the Priestesses gathering wood and then building bonfires, and Sigmund I want you to construct the cooking sections, and make sure you place one for roasting meat."

Sigmund looked surprised. "You were able to get meat from the Mattsons?"

"No, but the Jarl thankfully showed me someone else that could give us some."

"What about Britta?" Roose said, her smoky eyes piercing into hers.

"I hate that we are breaking up because of this," Teresa said.

"I do too, I wish it wasn't the case but it looks

like Britta will never accept the changes I will bring. I will deal with her."

Teresa grabbed her arm. "Don't be too harsh on her."

"I won't."

She couldn't, not at the moment. Sonja's new way still hadn't been tested. But that would change with this harvest festival.

But how would she deal with Britta? Since Britta was Head Teacher she had control over what the Acolytes did. If Britta wanted to she could make sure there were scroll teachings at the time of the harvest festival. It was crucial that the Acolytes attended. Sonja believed that Acolytes meeting the wider wagon train at the festival was crucial in changing the faith. They were the future of it after all.

Sonja stepped into the teaching wagon. It was a wide and long wagon, with desks placed in rows. White robed boys and girls sat at hard wooden chairs. They stood when Sonja walked in. All the children bowed to her. At the far end of the wagon, standing behind a lectern, Britta gave her a narrowed eyed stare.

Sonja walked down the classroom, smiling and nodding to the kids. She wanted to act as if this was a normal visit from the Keeper. She had an advantage in this setting as she was sure that Britta would try not to argue against her too much with kids watching. Still, her heart pounded and her mouth felt dry.

"Head Teacher Britta," she said, as bright and cheery as she could muster. "I have been told that you kept the Acolytes away from helping with the setup of the harvest festival. I feel the work given to them would help build teamwork."

"I felt that this festival might be too adult for them. It would be best for them to not be corrupted by what they see, so I decided that teaching scrolls would be a much better activity," Britta said, smiling a fake cheery smile.

"And may I ask what you are teaching the children?"

"The Scroll of Priest Robin's Account," Britta replied.

Of course she was. Before Robin was a Priest he was a farmer within the city of Elv. A city that he claimed was full of shadow and debauchery. One of the key descriptions in the scroll were the debauched and lewd parties the city's elite participated in. And Britta had claimed the harvest festival was too adult.

A boy at the front row put up his hand. "Miss Keeper, can I ask why you are putting on a party when Priest Robin said they are bad and full of shadow."

Britta put her hand on the lectern, and smiled. "Yes, Keeper, it might be good to explain to the Acolytes why it appears you are going against the Scrolls."

She gave a side eye glance to Britta, but turned to face the Acolytes. If Britta was going to fight, Sonja was going to fight back. "It's all to do with interpretation, my children. Now you all have been taught what it says in the scroll, how Priest Robin talks about the lewd parties, but also the waste of food within the city, and the corruption of the people in power."

"Now Priest Robin connects the parties with the corruption, but I think it has things the wrong way around. It isn't the parties that are causing the shadow, the parties are just a symptom of the corruption of those in power. The leaders of Elv only care about things like having a good time, which means having a lot of drink and food."

"But if you had a sensible leadership that wasn't so corrupt then the parties wouldn't be so excessive. Instead it would be a chance to bring joy and light to people, and bring them together as one. That is what I hope to do with this harvest festival."

The girls and boys sat at the desks all nodded their heads at this, making Sonja smile. Britta looked angry, and said in a loud voice. "Well yes, that's one interpretation, but another interpretation is that the parties did lead to corruption."

"Well that's the beauty of the scrolls, you can interpret them in a myriad of ways. That's why I want the Acolytes to come to the harvest festival and see for themselves whether your or my interpretation is valid. I want them to make their own minds up."

Britta grasped at the lectern. "You can't have children at an adult party."

"It is not an adult party, it is a party for everyone. As a Keeper I have decreed that these Acolytes are going to it.

She gave Britta a hard stare, daring her to defy what she just said. There was some cheering and whooping from the children, so Britta stepped back and bowed her head.

Sonja felt satisfaction at being able to beat Britta, it died away when she saw that Britta was only just containing her fury.

The two of them had been such close friends. Sonja's fondest moment had been when Britta received the role of Head Teacher. Sonja's proudest moment had been when Britta gave her a hug and said congratulations after she received the role of General.

She leaned forwards, whispering, "Why do we have to fight like this?"

Britta gave her a hard stare. "Because you are going to destroy this faith."

Britta strode out of the classroom. Sonja watched her go, tears in her eyes. Was she on the right path, were the changes to the faith worth the destruction of her and Britta's friendship?

But she remembered the underlying sadness she had felt when she had been friends with Britta. It wasn't Britta's fault really, she had been a ray of sunshine within dark clouds. But the way the faith obsessed about being pure made Sonja feel ashamed about her feelings and actions. Britta acted so perfect and pure, she didn't have any sexual thoughts about other women, she didn't go to parties to drink and overeat. She was always so loved by their mother. Sonja asked herself why she couldn't just be like Britta? Why was Britta so much better than her? Those questions just brought her down a path of self destruction.

Sonja looked out at the Acolytes, and saw the girl with the blond curly hair that she had comforted about her gay feelings. The girl gave her a big smile. Sonja smiled back.

She would no longer let others go along her path of misery and destruction. There was a new path she was going to create for these children. And if that meant having to get rid of Britta to create that path, then so be it.

IF YOU VISIT EIK, MAKE SURE IT'S AROUND SPRING. THE CITIES SPRING FESTIVAL IS A COLOURFUL DELIGHT, FILLED WITH DRINK, DANCE, AND A COMMUNITY COMING TOGETHER

'Travel Guide For Eik' by Gabriela Than

The storage wagons in Bonde Square were filled to bursting with bags of oats, wheat, and sugar, which sat next to boxes of carrots, cucumbers, potatoes, lettuces, and all manner of other vegetables. The farmers had stopped wiping sweat off their brows. Now was the time to celebrate a good job done, and talk to one another. And what they talked about most was the coming harvest festival.

A buzz of excitement sparked between all the farmer's. There was surprise that the faith was the one holding the festival, and along with the surprise was a question on whether the festival would be any good. Many had opinions about it, and these opinions would turn to theories about why the faith was really setting up this celebration. Many felt it had to be a ploy.

Sigrun had joined these groups, and

participated in the discussions. She had to be seen to be one of the people, not a Jarl on high. Even though she knew they participated in Hannes' army and wanted to overthrow the faith, the group she found herself in the most was the one with Thore, Daniel, and Aina.

When she walked towards them, Thore had given her a narrowed look. The air between them was initially frosty. Everyone had gone quiet.

"You know I'm not wearing that fancy cloak or tunic anymore," she said to them.

"You're still the Jarl," Thore replied.

"Hannes was a Jarl and you seemed to get on with him, what's the difference?"

"Hannes didn't try to act better than us, or fool us," Aina said.

Sigrun looked down at her muddy tunic and frayed trousers. "I definitely don't think I'm higher than you. In fact I respect what you do and think the wagon train should be listening to what you want more often. Little people don't get a say around here enough."

Daniel looked impressed by that, but Thore wasn't too sure. "It's easy to say that, but you got to prove it."

She put up her hands. "Well here I am, trying

to prove it. What would you like to see happen in the wagon train?"

It didn't totally warm the group to her, but at least she got several opinions thrown at her: more breaks at work, better repairs for their wagons, or stopping the wagon train at some nice spot in the world to settle down. She made sure to listen, and told them that she would see what she could do.

The discussion eventually got to the harvest festival and the level of excitement people had. Sigrun was a little curious why this group had so much excitement when they had gone to parties every week, and asked as such.

"Well this party is different," Thore said. "This is a celebration of our work. The other parties are just us trying to forget work."

"I'm curious, do you like all the food you harvest going to those weekly parties you attend?. Seems like a lot of work for a lot of food to go to waste."

Daniel seemed to think about that. Aina scratched her chin. "Well it ain't a party without some food in it."

"You might be right, I've not thought about it," Thore said. "But I like going to those parties for the sociable aspects."

She nodded. "I understand that."

But she said no more, not wanting to push her views too far. It was a delicate process trying to convince people of your way of thinking, too many people hammered it in, which usually pushed people to reject it. But her method allowed people to think about the issues, and start to come to conclusions on their own about them. But she did think that with a little bit of pushing she could get the people on board with her law on limiting parties.

After a while of being in Thore's group, she said goodbye and went to another group. She made sure to go to every group that was standing around Bonde Square. It was important to try to listen to them all, and to show them that she was their Jarl. She also wanted to make them think about the weekly parties. For some groups it only took a few jokes or comments to get them on board. For others the atmosphere still felt a little icy when she left. Those she was disappointed with, but she made sure to make a note of them so she could warm them up the next time. She wouldn't be able to change everyone's minds today, but there was always tomorrow.

The one thing that was clear going from group

to group, was that the anticipation was building for the harvest festival. Everyone looked up in the sky and commented how Manang was moving too slowly, and couldn't it be the evening yet?

Sigrun herself thought of Sonja, wondering how she was dealing with the stress of organizing a festival that everyone in the wagon train was probably going to attend. The two of them hadn't seen each other since she stormed off in Kveg Plain. She felt guilty about that, and hoped that there was some point in the evening that she could say she was sorry.

At that thought, she said goodbye to the farmers, and went down Blomst Street. Sonja had given her a lovely rose the last time they had seen each other, so Sigrun had to return the favor. She glanced on both sides of the streets, marveling at the hanging baskets that contained colorful flowers. The sweet and pungent aromas almost overwhelmed her, but there was one smell that grabbed her and steered her towards its flower. The smell reminded Sigrun of her mother as it smelled of peach. The flower was bright yellow and looked a lot like the spokes of a windmill. She felt it was the perfect gift for Sonja, as it looked to be the same color as the faithful robes. She carefully picked it up from the basket.

She put the windmill flower in her pocket, and slowly wandered down Blomst Street. The air felt warm, and the sky was a bright blue. Sigrun whistled a merry tune, feeling like it was a good day to hold a harvest festival.

***

Manang slowly sunk into the horizon, painting the sky red and purple. Sonja gazed over the field and marveled at its transformation. There were hundreds of tables of various shapes and sizes dotted about, with chairs arrayed around them. In between the seating were roaring bonfires. At the far end there were three roasting spits, spinning beef, lamb, and pork, and these were next to a metal oven – donated kindly by Yael Hoademaker. Sigmund was currently using the oven to roast veg, and fry sausages.

Everything looked perfect. Yes the meats were slightly small and would probably go within the first hour, but she felt that people would be impressed that they even had some.

The only thing that marred the work on the field, was the fact that Britta and her handful of Priests and Priestesses were standing in the middle of it. They were shouting scripture from Priest Robin's Account. They told the faithful the festival was a grave shadow and how they should all be ashamed of themselves for participating in it.

Most faithful looked over to Britta and her crew with some embarrassment. One Priest even went up to Sonja and asked whether he could get rid of her. Sonja thought about it for a bit, but in the end said no.

She very much would like to get rid of Britta, but physically dragging her away would do more damage than she was currently causing. Everyone could ignore her at the moment. The one worry was what the wider wagon train would think of Britta. Would they be disappointed, feel this was typical of the faithful, and go somewhere else, or would they ignore it like the faithful were, and try to have a good time to spite her. There wasn't really much Sonja could do about it, as she guessed Britta wanted to be manhandled to show them how evil her path was. She just had to hope that the festival goers would find the allure of the party more powerful.

The faithful sat on the yellow wood pews, waiting for Manang to disappear under the horizon. There was a nervous energy crackling about the Priests, Priestesses, and Acolytes. Everyone was waiting for a throng of people to come in, and the festivities to begin.

Sonja felt now was the best time to tell them the ground rules of the festival. She slapped her hands, and everyone turned. The pews quickly became quiet, except for the shouts of Britta in the background.

"I know we are all excited about this harvest festival. But this will be a strange experience for all of you. You won't have experienced this much food being eaten or drink being consumed, and a part of you is going to feel that it's all wrong. I understand that, but you must let the party continue. But that doesn't mean everything you see is ok. If you see people are too drunk, or are starting to do lewd things, you have my permission to stop them.

"Now, you have to be delicate about how you do that. I don't want people to feel we are being like the old faith, demanding they do things our way. I think you can be gentle and quietly push them out. Try to convince them that what they are doing is better in some other party."

"The other thing I ask, nay demand, is that you join in on this feast. I don't want any Priest,

Priestess, or Acolyte standing at the side of the field watching the people as they have fun. You need to join in on the fun, talk to people at the tables, dance with people around the fireplace, maybe Priests and Priestesses have a bit of a drink yourself. This party is all about bringing us and the wagon train together. That can't be done unless you actually get together."

Everyone clapped and cheered, and the buzz of energy electrified everyone anew. Most faithful talked about how fun that evening's festivities were going to be, and how excited they were to talk to new people.

Sonja smiled as she heard all of this, feeling the warmth in the air. She watched as Manang dipped lower and lower in the horizon. The sky turned inky black, and the stars twinkled into life.

***

The party atmosphere was in full swing, and Sigrun was the life of it. She stood next to tables, eating food, chatting and laughing with the guests. She danced around the bonfires, inhaling the heady smoke and spinning around with men and women. She kept going back to the barrels of mead, taking out another pint, and was still surprised she was drinking in the middle of the faith's encampment.

Sigrun didn't just stick around worker groups. After all this was supposed to be a party of unity - Sonja had made a speech about it being such at the start of the festivities - so she made sure to hang around the groups of yellow robed Priests and Priestesses as well. She drank more and more. The stars streaked across the sky, and the orange of the bonfires were getting fuzzy.

Around the faithful she asked more and more questions. Why did they think that Sol was coming back, what was the Mission really all about, what did they think about all this partying when they had put their nose down on it just a few months ago? Unfortunately, she was a little too drunk to remember the answers.

Still, she nodded, smiled, and laughed. It seemed to do the trick. Soon a gaggle of yellow robed men and women followed her over to the bonfire, and danced around. Some of them were cute women, but she had eyes for only one woman now.

It was a shame. Sigrun could probably have some fun with these women, and open some eyes to alternative ways of love, but she didn't want to hurt Sonja and risk losing her. So she made sure the dances were always at a respectable distance, and the conversations never got too flirty.

In outward appearance Sigrun was like her old self: confident, cocky, and always drunk. But as the night went on, inwardly she felt a little lonely and lost. She had fun with these priests, priestesses, and wagon train workers, but it always felt like something was missing.

Sigrun kept glancing towards the tables, in the hopes of seeing Sonja. Whenever she did, she felt a little boost of confidence and happiness, which allowed her to go on. But when she didn't see her, she felt sad, and her chat or dance fell a little flat. Socializing with all these people was important, but near the end Sigrun just wanted to find a quiet little corner with Sonja to talk.

As the evening went on, the party became more wild. Workers danced a little closer to one another, their bodies gyrating in time to the music. The faithful looked at this with shock, and rushed over to gently steer them away from the party. Some people found this unacceptable, and shouted at the faithful they were taking away their freedoms, but they were soon pushed out into the darkness.

Seeing this, Sigrun stopped drinking. Usually at this point of the party she would have been close to blacking out, but her heart wasn't into drinking excessively anymore. Eventually, after visiting every bonfire and sitting down at every table, her heart wasn't in being sociable either. All her thoughts were on talking to Sonja alone. She checked her pocket to see if the windmill flower was still there, and went to find her.

As she got closer to the center of the field, she heard the shouts of the curly haired Priestess. One bizarre thing about the festival was that a group of faithful had shouted throughout how the party was an abomination, and how every participant was full of shadow for participating. Most people in the wagon train had expected this from the faithful, but had been surprised when others in the faith told them that what the woman shouted wasn't what they thought, and that the workers should ignore it. Once the music started, this wasn't too hard.

Yet the woman was still here while the sky was dark purple and the stars were twinkling. She still shouted about shadow, while men and women staggered out of the field being sick. It felt like if the party was still here in the morning then the woman would be as well. The curly haired woman gave Sigrun an evil look when she passed, which she ignored.

Sigrun snaked through tables, searching the darkness for any sign of Sonja. She saw her flame robes by the empty spit roast. Sonja stood alone.

"The meat didn't last too long," Sigrun said, feeling it was a lame thing to say to someone you hadn't seen for a few days.

However, Sonja still smiled, which boosted Sigrun's mood.

"But the people ate it gratefully anyway and didn't complain when it was gone," Sonja said, nodding. "I thank you for getting it for me."

"Least I could do."

She stared at Sonja's dark hair and narrow face, which she found beautiful. God she wanted to kiss her right now. Sigrun glanced behind, all she could see was the inky black sky with a few dots of blazing orange. The only sounds were the crackle of the fire, and the distant shouts from the curly haired woman. Would anyone see the two of them kiss?

"I got you a present," she said, carefully taking out the windmill flower from her pocket.

"You really didn't need to get me anything. Obtaining the meat for me was enough," Sonja said, but her face looked delighted and curious.

Sigrun spun the windmill flower around, the yellow glinting in the firelight. Sonja's face lit up. She took the flower, and grabbed Sigrun for a hug.

They broke their embrace, too soon in Sigrun's eyes. They were very close but acted awkward. Sigrun glanced around the field. However her desire to kiss Sonja was too great and she threw caution to the wind. She grabbed Sonja's hand, and kissed her.

The kiss was as joyous and explosive as any other, but much too brief. Sonja pushed Sigrun away and glanced around the field in terror.

"We can't, someone might see."

Sigrun stepped forwards. "I don't care. I want you. I don't want to wait anymore."

"This festival will be seen as a success, the path will be laid for the faithful to change. We will be together soon."

"How long is soon, months, years? There's a woman in the middle shouting about how partying is a shadow. If she is shouting about partying she would never accept you being gay. The faithful aren't going to change anytime soon."

"I disagree. And if you want to be with me, you'll wait," Sonja said, voice stern.

"What would happen if they knew, if they saw me kissing you now?" she asked.

"It wouldn't just be a woman shouting, it would be them throwing stones, dragging me out of the Sol Shards protection, and watching me freeze to death."

Sigrun raised her eyebrows. "And you are saying you can change them from that reaction to acceptance?"

Sonja bit her lip. "That's all I can hope for."

"Why are you putting the effort in? Why do you care so much about these people? Who would rather have you killed than be happily in love with another woman."

"Because, like it or not, this is my home. I consider these people my family. I love them and I love Sol. And I have seen them and the wagon train come together with our love. So trust me, and wait."

"What do you mean you have seen them and the wagon train come together with our love?" she asked.

Sonja sighed, and said, "When I was near to it I felt the Sol Shard call to me. I held it in my hands, and saw a vision. In it the wagon train was divided in the middle. There were two sides: the faithful and the non faithful, and they were ready to go to war. But I walked between them with my friends, and they stopped to look. You were there at the Keeper's podium, and we were both dressed in white. The two of us shared union vows. We kissed, causing a bright light to be cast out. That light made the people in the wagon train drop their swords and cheer. What the vision was telling me was clear: our union will bring the wagon train together."

Sigrun didn't know whether Sonja was crazy, seeing visions of a bright light coming from a kiss definitely fit the bill, but the idea of the two of them sharing union vows was definitely very appealing. At the thought of it, Sigrun felt warmth in her heart.

"You don't believe me, do you?" Sonja said, stepping back.

Sigrun stepped forwards. "I've never believed in visions, and I don't know if I believe in Sol, but I believe in you. It feels like you are taking this vision seriously, so I guess I have to believe that you saw it. I won't deny the things you said sound lovely. I wouldn't mind it if they came true."

"So you'll wait?"

She sighed. "I can wait."

Sigrun felt a stab in her heart at the idea of waiting, but she didn't want to hurt Sonja or risk losing her. If it was between feeling sad but having the occasional joy versus feeling sad all the time, she would pick the former all the time.

"But can we still find somewhere private, so I can properly kiss you?" she asked.

Sonja grabbed her hand, and pulled her away. They ran through the inky blackness, laughing as they went. The two of them rushed through the warm air, staring into each other's eyes.

"I think I love you," Sigrun said, as natural as the stars twinkling above.

Sonja grinned. "I think I love you too."

Part Three

Sharp Enough To Stab

THERE WAS ONE TIME I HAD TO HIDE IN A WHOLE CART OF FISH TO AVOID THE GUARDS

'The Heroic Exploits Of Thomasina' by Bacchus Vinay

Sonja woke up, her arm numb. Sigrun's bed wasn't big enough for two people, not to mention the fact that it was lumpy and uncomfortable. She had to sleep sideways while Sigrun hogged the bed, being pushed to the edges of the bed and onto the wall. It was good that she loved Sigrun, otherwise she probably would have hit her for making her uncomfortable.

Sonja's mouth was dry. She had a headache, and felt a little ill. She had drunk too much last night. Only in her teenage years had she drunk that much.

Feeling Sigrun's naked skin with the back of her hand made her feel better. She felt she could stay cuddled up to Sigrun, staring at her messy blond hair and knotted braid forever. Unfortunately, someone banged on the door.

The bang was violent enough to judder the whole wagon. She feared that the door would burst open. Sigrun groaned and stirred, but she wasn't getting up. Sonja sat up and was going to go to the door to see who it was but then realized that she wasn't meant to be in this wagon, and if she was seen people would know about her and Sigrun's relationship. So instead of going to the door, Sonja shook Sigrun until she groaned some more.

"What is it?" Sigrun said.

"Someone really wants to see you," she replied.

Sigrun groaned again, and slowly put her feet onto the floor below. She yawned and stretched, allowing Sonja to appreciate her naked body

The person behind the door kept banging on and on. Sigrun furrowed her brow. "I'm coming."

Sigrun quickly dressed in the clothes she wore at the party. Sonja put the covers over her to hide, but left a small gap so she could see who was at the door. Her stomach dropped when Sigrun opened the door and it was revealed to be Britta.

"What are you doing here?" Sigrun asked.

Britta narrowed her eyes. "Where is the Keeper?"

"How should I know, probably in her wagon sleeping off the party last night."

"Don't lie, I saw you two running off together," Britta said, trying to peer into the wagon.

Sonja cursed not being careful when they ran off. They had been at a party, of course someone could have seen them. But as soon as she had cursed herself another part of her chided herself for doing so. Why couldn't she just be together with another woman? Why did she have to keep hiding who she was? She had vowed not to do that anymore, but here she was doing exactly that. Maybe Sigrun had been right last night, maybe she would be waiting forever for the faith to be ready for the truth.

Sigrun stepped in front of Britta. "I think the darkness and the craziness of the party has gotten you confused. Maybe you saw some other women running away, it's been known to happen."

Britta raised your voice. "I know you're in there Sonja, stop being a coward and face your shadow head on. Maybe Sol might just forgive you."

"Right, if you're done shouting can you kindly go back to your encampment," Sigrun said, annoyance clear in her voice.

Britta pushed Sigrun, and scrambled around, getting into the wagon for a brief second. Sonja's heart pounded, and she stopped moving. Sigrun forcefully wrapped her arm around Britta's side and pushed her back through the door. Britta stumbled backwards, but righted herself.

"Ok, you can seriously fuck off now," Sigrun shouted.

Britta gave her another narrowed eyed stare, shook her head, and walked off into the faith encampment. Sigrun sighed, and shut the door.

Sonja threw off her covers. "This is not good."

"I got rid of her."

"Yes, but the problem is I'm still here."

Sigrun looked at her confused.

Sonja quickly got up from the bed, and slipped on her flame robe. "The faithful are going to expect me to come out of the Keeper's wagon this morning. If instead I am seen coming from the edges of the faith encampment, that gives credence to what Britta is going to shout to them. She might even convince a lot of them that I slept with you last night."

"Ah," Sigrun said, grimacing.

"So how do I go from here to my wagon, which is in the middle of the faith encampment and can be seen by many people, without being seen?" she asked, feeling frustrated that she had to be in this position.

Sigrun walked around her wagon for any

answers, and then put a finger on the wheelbarrow that was under the shelf of books. "We will use this."

Sonja walked over to inspect it. The wheelbarrow was long enough to fit in, if she bent her legs a little. They would just have to put something over it so she would be hidden. She climbed in, and Sigrun put her bed cover over it.

"Is it any good?" Sonja asked.

"I can't see you, but I'm sure the faith will be suspicious. I'm bringing a wheelbarrow into their place with a bed cover on," Sigrun said, shaking her head.

Sonja sighed. It really wasn't a great plan, but it seemed to be all they had. She wanted the faith to change, to be able to accept her as she truly was, but she didn't feel springing in onto them now would be a good thing. If she was going to change them and be herself then she had to do it in the right way.

"Just tell them you have come over to help with the clear up of the festival, and you are wanting to speak to me to get my permission to do it," she said.

"And the bed cover?"

"Just say it's to make sure the wheelbarrow is

protected, or for small debris, or something."

Sigrun gave a 'this isn't going to work' glance at Sonja. "Well, you can't say our relationship isn't interesting."

Sonja felt every tip, turn, and judder of the wheelbarrow in her body as it wheeled across the grass. It was warm under the cover, and the air was stale. She felt claustrophobic, and she had a strong desire to constantly peek her head out so she could get some fresh air and light. She fought the instinct, breathing in and out to calm herself.

Sonja started to hear the faint sound of people from afar. Even though she couldn't see anything, she thought the barrow had passed across the encampment threshold. With only a few pushes to go she would be at her wagon.

The wheelbarrow suddenly stopped, and she had to hold on to not fall out. She wanted to ask what had happened but realized she couldn't. She inwardly sighed, hating that she was reduced to sneaking into her own encampment in a wheelbarrow. If someone wrote the history of her Keepership would they mention this tale? There would definitely be bursts of laughter for whoever heard it.

"Jarl Sigrun, what are you doing in here with a wheelbarrow," a male voice said. It sounded like Sigmund.

"I've come to help you clear up," Sigrun said in her cheery voice.

Even though it was embarrassing, Sonja still felt warmth in her heart at the fact that Sigrun was going out of her way to help her. A lot of people could have just said it was her mess to sort out, but not Sigrun. She understood how important it was to Sonja to do this and so made sure to do everything she could to make it happen. It made Sonja appreciate and love Sigrun that much more.

"I don't know," Sigmund said. "Usually Acolytes get given that job."

"Tch, getting kids to do all your hard work, what kind of faith is this?" Sigrun said.

"Still, I can't really say whether you can or can't."

Sonja felt that Sigmund was being a bit too rules focused and hesitant, but in this case she thanked him as it allowed Sigrun to come to the subject of the Keeper.

"Well then I will just have to ask the person who can," Sigrun said. "I'll wheel this to the

Keeper."

"You sure you don't want me to keep hold of the wheelbarrow for you?" Sigmund asked.

"Oh definitely not."

The wheelbarrow raised again, and it shuddered off into the faith encampment. Sonja breathed out in relief. This wasn't going so badly.

And then she heard a shout from Britta. "What are you doing here, Jarl, with a wheelbarrow?"

They picked up speed. Sigrun shouted back, "No time to chat, I got an important talk with the Keeper."

Sonja could hear the wheel rolling across the grass, and the sound of boots running towards them. Sigrun muttered under her breath, "Am I going to make it, am I going to make it, am I going to..."

The wheelbarrow turned sharply, and Sonja nearly fell out. She put her hand up to save herself, and felt wood.

"I'll distract her," Sigrun whispered. "Get out, and run around the wagon."

Sonja did as she was told. She carefully peeled the cover off herself. She emerged at the west side of the Keeper's wagon. Sigrun and Britta stood around the corner.

"I know you are trying to hide the Keeper in that wheelbarrow," Britta said.

"You really have an active imagination," Sigrun replied.

Sonja ran around the Keeper's wagon. She walked to the front, where the pews and the podium were. She glanced around the area, deserted. She breathed out, feeling like she had been lucky, opened the door of the wagon, and ran in.

The voices of Sigrun and Britta drew nearer to the door. Sonja smoothed her hair and the flame robe, breathed in, and opened it.

"What a pleasant surprise to see you Jarl Sigrun, what brings you here," she said, hoping that she was talking in her best Keeper voice.

Britta glanced between her and Sigrun. "Come on, you can't expect me to believe this can you?"

"I don't know what you believe, Britta," she said, smiling sweetly. Now she truly wanted to drag Britta by her curly hair and throw her out of the encampment for what had happened today.

"Yes, I'm just here to help clean up the mess of the festival," Sigrun added.

Sonja nodded her head. "I thank you for the gesture, but that won't be necessary."

Britta gave them one last hard stare. "I know what happened and I'm going to tell everyone."

She walked off, shouting to anyone that was close about how the Keeper was full of shadow. Sonja watched her go, shaking her head and breathing a sigh of relief.

"Well, that was quite fun," Sigrun said, looking up at Sonja and grinning. "Let me know when you want to sneak into a place with a wheelbarrow again."

"I think next time you should have a go," Sonja said, laughing at the absurdity of it all. She bent down and whispered, "I thank you anyway for doing that. You truly saved me."

Sigrun nodded to her. "Anytime, my Keeper."

Sigrun took hold of the wheelbarrow, and wheeled it away, giving Sonja a wave. Sonja watched her go, feeling warmth within her heart but also a little sadness. She had really wanted to spend that morning in bed with Sigrun, snuggling up to her and not caring about the faith or the wagon train. But Britta had ruined all of that.

She gripped her hands, feeling all the frustration and embarrassment of that morning in one go. She was sick and tired of having to hide herself, and she was sick and tired of Britta making her life difficult. Both of them had to be dealt with.

THERE IS TRUE SATISFACTION WITH GETTING YOUR LAW PASSED INTO STATUTE, ESPECIALLY BECAUSE YOU KNOW HOW MUCH WORK IT TOOK TO DO SO

'Lawyered Up' by Sel Sitai

Sigrun couldn't help smirk in amusement about what had happened with Sonja. The sequence of events: having to wheelbarrow her across the faith's encampment, running away from Britta, and pretending that she didn't know what Britta was talking about, seemed absurd in the warm sun. She understood the seriousness of what would happen if Sonja was caught being with her, but she couldn't help but see the comedy in how they went about hiding it. All morning she kept flashing back to the misadventure, and laughed.

For most of the walk through the wagon train she was alone, apart from the occasional horse trotting across the street. Because of the festival last night, the wagon train was slow to wake up. Many bosses treated this as a day of rest, and many workers used it to their full advantage.

As she got nearer to Bonde Square, men and women started to step out of their wagons. They brought out a chair and table, a pack of cards or kings game board, while their friends or neighbors that joined them brought a small bottle of gin, whiskey, or rum. Soon, the wagon train was full of casual chatter, laughter, and casual competition. Sigrun smiled to see the train like this, so much so that she whistled a tune while striding past.

She didn't know why she found herself coming to Bonde Square so often, why it was the farmers she talked to the most, but strangely it felt the most natural. Maybe it was because the farmers were the true heart of the place. Sure, it was the Mission that decided on the destination most of the time, but it was the farmers that they relied on to survive. Sure, the Hoademakers put clothes on their bodies, and the Mattsons cooked the food, but if the worst came to the worst they could live without those families for a spell or find replacements. But they would never find a replacement for the farmers. They had honed their skills in planting, tending, and harvesting crops within a moving caravan. It felt like they should be the most well treated.

Manang blazed down a glorious reddish light onto Bonde Square. Many of the carts that had contained crops had been moved to the side, and the vast grassy expanse was now filled with various tables, chairs, and barrels full of beer. The wind had a cold spring freshness, meaning the farmers sitting or standing wore thicker tunics, or sometimes wrapped blankets around their shoulders as makeshift cloaks.

Sigrun did not wear a cloak anymore, nor her fancy tunic. She wore her muddy tunic and trousers, and wore it with pride. When she strode in, many of the groups waved to her or smiled as she passed. She smiled back, feeling like she was herself again. She would have to thank Joan profusely for her advice. Being herself was the best political move she had made as Jarl.

But she wasn't here to see Joan or Gregor, though that might come later. No, she was here to explain her new law to the people of the wagon train.

She glanced at the men and women who sat at tables or stood near beer barrels. Would they accept sacrificing their fun every week? All she could do was hope so, if not then she would have to find some other way to stop Hannes. And the other ways could be fraught with a lot more danger.

The farmers shouted to her that last night had

been a good festival, that they were surprised the faith put on such a good party, and that they appreciated her for being such a good dancer or person to talk to. She couldn't help but smile at the last part. She would have to remember to tell Sonja the farmers thought the party had been a great success. Sonja would definitely feel joy about her plan succeeding.

Sigrun stopped at each group of farmers to chat a little, but eventually she told them that she had something to say and that they should all gather around in a circle. Eventually the message spread around, and the farmers all bunched up in the square.

A group of important Baldurs with Sven as the leader, got curious about this and walked up to her. Sven had his usual smile on his face, but there was a hint of worry and sadness within his eyes. There definitely seemed to be something serious going on with the Baldurs.

"What's this all about?" Sven asked.

"You and your farmers are going to be the first to hear my announcement of a new law. I've come here personally to explain the merits of it and get the people's approval."

"Ah, my mother told me about this," Sven said,

scratching his chin. "Is now a good time to announce it though. Most people here just want to chill and rest, they don't want to think about politics."

"Now is a perfect time, most people are happy about the festival last night so my explanation will have the most impact," she said, giving him a smile.

Sven examined her, seeming to wonder whether he should allow this to happen. Sigrun felt a little annoyed at that, wasn't she Jarl, didn't that mean she could do things how she wanted to do them?

But she resisted the urge to tell Sven this. If the rumors about Gregor's ill health were to be believed it wouldn't be too long before she would have to deal with Sven. It was good to keep any potential political relationship as happy as possible, just so it wasn't too difficult to get what you wanted from them. It was a shame she couldn't have a similar relationship with the Mattsons.

"It'll only take a few moments of people's time, and then you can all go back to your chilling," she said.

Sven nodded. He and his important brothers

and cousins stepped back into the crowd. Many farmers had watched the exchange with curiosity, but there were a few here and there that were fidgeted and looked bored. She would have to talk quicker now.

"Men and women that farm the fields, I first have to thank you for all the work you did for the harvest. This wagon train literally wouldn't survive without you, and I feel we don't appreciate you enough for it. It shouldn't be those Hoademakers with the fancy tunics and cloaks, it should be all of you wearing them for the work you do. But then again those tunics might get a bit muddy with all that digging in the dirt."

There were a lot of proud looks and nods as she spoke, and the last line got a good laugh. She smiled, feeling in her element. She had never spoken to a whole crowd of people before, never tried to explain herself and why she was doing a certain action. As a cattle rancher she had mostly been on her own, doing her own thing, and never really interacting with others for that long. And yet here she was, standing in the middle of a circle of people staring at her, and she felt confident. In fact, she felt more than confident, she felt like she could be the best damn Jarl this wagon train had ever seen. All she would have to do was get on with the work and bring the people along.

"Last night the faithful held a party in your honor. We ate the fruits of your labor, drank to your sweat and toil, and had a few crazy dances along the way. But it was more than a celebration, we came together last night as a wagon train. Two sides that had been divided drove on the road to eventually heal wounds. That is important, and I have to thank the Mission of Sol for being brave enough to step forwards to try to heal those wounds."

There was a cheer for that, and many raised a glass to the faith and drank their beer. Sigrun would have to let Sonja know about that.

"It's events like those which make me positive about the wagon train's future. If we could have more parties that allowed us to come together, then our little bit of the world would be happy and carefree. The only issues we would have to care about would be raiders, or merchants selling goods for way too much money."

Another smattering of laughter. Her heart was racing now, this was her moment, this was where she would tell them her law.

"But the parties like the festival we had last night are not the only parties we have. There are many weekly parties, ones involving feasting, drinking, and more carnal activities. These aren't parties that are about people coming together, not really, these are events about forgetting your work and your troubles, drowning out your world with excessive drinking and food. Food I might add you worked all season to nurture, to grow, and to harvest.

"And yet I've seen what happens to that food, it gets piled up on tables, eaten a little, and then chucked away. Do you really want all that hard labor to be wasted like that?"

"I feel your work deserves better, I think you deserve better. We should stop these weekly parties, stop the waste of food. We should have parties that are meaningful to the wagon train, that bring people together, and that project a happy and carefree future. And that is why I am bringing a law that will do just that. There will only be a set amount of parties in the year, which will have food and drink, but that will be controlled. We need to make sure we can survive the future, we need to make sure your hard work doesn't go to waste."

She breathed in, feeling a little exhausted saying so much. The crowd was silent, staring at her, probably processing what she had just said. Sigrun glanced at the faces around the circle, and couldn't tell what their reaction was going to be. Were they going to accept this, completely reject it, or would it be mixed? She just wanted someone to woop or throw a cup at her.

But eventually someone did say something. Daniel, the young man in the group of farmers she hung about with, stepped forwards. "Those parties are our way of letting our hair down. Yes they aren't noble, but that's not what they are for. You can't get rid of one of the outlets we use to get away from our hard jobs."

There were a few nods and shouts of agreement to that. It didn't surprise Sigrun, she was expecting the argument.

She put up her hands. "I totally get that. You deserve to have relief from all your hard work. That's why, along with this party plan, I am also bringing in a law that will give you a day off work. At the moment you get breaks and half an afternoon, but you deserve more than that."

Sven narrowed his eyes at that. Yeah, she was going against the Baldur's wishes somewhat but she felt she had to. And the appreciative nods and cheers from people in the crowd let her know that it had been a worthwhile gamble. Even though Sven would grumble and mutter how it was a bad idea, they wouldn't actively go against it. Like they hadn't actively gone against the weekly parties, even though they knew how damaging they were. At least her proposal wasn't as damaging.

She looked at the crowd. "I appreciate that this is a big change that I'm proposing, that I'm taking away something that a lot of you have enjoyed. I truly believe I am doing something right, that I am benefiting the wagon train, and more importantly I'm benefiting you and your work. But I also know that you will all see problems that I don't see. It will be a few days before the council votes on this law, so I want anyone that has a problem or wants something tweaked to come to me and say what that is. I am open to listening to you, and changing things based on your ideas, because that's what it's all about at the end of the day: making you happy."

She nodded to the crowd. There were whoops and cheers as she walked through the throng. Many hands clapped her on the back or shouted their appreciation. She couldn't help but grin, and thank them back. Her attitude had gone down well, and she was feeling that sense of greatness again. She could be the greatest Jarl of them all.

Sigrun knew that it wasn't over, that she would probably have many that would come to her with problems and suggestions for changes. There was also the vote itself. Even though she had fulfilled her end of the bargain to Gregor, that didn't guarantee her success. Maybe Gregor, or even Sven, would change their minds, hating the idea of a day off. Maybe Sonja wouldn't be able to convince her side to vote for the law.

But at least she made a step in the right direction, and at the moment everyone took it positively.

SEE THIS DAGGER, SEE HOW MANY ENEMIES I HAVE STABBED WITH THEE

Act 2, Scene 3 of 'Safiye II'

Sonja strode around the faith's encampment, waking up the Priests, Priestesses, and Acolytes. She gave them a cheery smile when they rubbed their eyes, and told them that they needed to clear the field up. Many groaned at this, but she told them it was necessary and that she would help them.

The scale of the task seemed overwhelming. There were tables and chairs to put back, burnt bonfire wood to dispose of, cooking implements to put away, and the detritus of the party to clear up, including bones, mugs, and in a weird case some clothes. It was a hard and hot job, especially with the red glow of Manang casting down on them and the warm wind blowing through. But by working together as a group, chatting, and singing songs, they were able to complete the tasks quickly.

During this work, Sonja had a rare chance to be with the faithful without them focusing on her. She had a chance to listen in on their conversations, understand what they truly thought about everything. The main topic of conversation was about the harvest festival.

One Priest and Priestess were surprised how fun dancing had been, and how they became friends with the others around the bonfire. A group of Priests had a deep conversation with some farmers about Sol and what would need to happen to bring her back into the sky. Some Acolytes played games with other kids, pretending to be duelists and attacking each other with sticks or jumping on tables. And a group of Priestess caught a couple kissing passionately - one woman thought they would have sex right there on the grass - but they had been surprised that the couple weren't violent when the Priestess tried to push them out the party, in fact they were very apologetic.

All these conversations buoyed Sonja's mood as the day went on. Her gamble had paid off. The faith was on the right track to change. Were they ready now for her secret? The positivity of the festival, and the fact that she was the one that organized it, could mean that the people wouldn't find her secret too damaging for the faith. They could see that someone that loved the same sex also brought happiness and positivity to their faith.

The only thing that stopped her was the fact that Britta still stood in the middle of the field shouting about shadow and the destruction of the faith. This time the arguments were about how she and Sigrun secretly loved each other.

"How can any of you accept someone that has a shadow that black to be your leader?" She shouted.

Many that were with Sonja told her that they didn't believe Britta anymore, and felt that Britta's path was a dead end for the faith. But even with these compliments, and even with the positivity of the festival going well, hearing Britta's accusation felt frustrating. Britta had been one of her best friends, the closest thing that she had to a sister, and now Britta saw her as a monster, almost as bad as Manang.

She tried to ignore the shouting, tried to ignore the little dagger in her heart every time Britta said that Sonja would cause the destruction of the faith because of her shadow filled ways, but eventually the protest burrowed into her brain enough. She couldn't allow Britta to have power in the faith anymore, to go against the changes she was making to the faith. If Britta was able to convince people that her methods would cause the destruction of the faith then Sonja would never be allowed to be her true self, and she was done hiding who she was. Britta had to be fired from her Head Teacher role.

But Sonja had to do it in a clever way. Even though many were on her side and didn't listen to Britta, it would still feel like she was getting rid of her because she didn't like what she said. Even if the suspicion wasn't that big it would put doubt in people's minds about how Sonja used her power, and if there were more Britta's in the future and she fired them as well her abuse of power would start to look like a pattern. She had to find a way for Britta's firing to look reasonable, like Sonja was getting rid of her for something else other than the opinion.

After she had gathered the burnt bits of firewood and put it in the wheelbarrow. She straightened herself up, breathed in a little, preparing herself for the conversation with her former friend, and strode up to Britta.

Britta shouted louder. "Here comes the shadow filled Keeper. I wonder whether she will want to kill me or kiss me."

Sonja rolled her eyes at that. "Britta, I have a

change I need you to make. We can talk about this privately in my wagon."

"No, the conversation will happen here, in front of everyone," Britta said, holding up her hands and smiling.

Britta obviously understood she was going to fire her, wanting the crowd to see her being attacked for her views. But Britta would not get what she wanted.

"Ok then, I'll say it here," she said, breathing in and out a little. "I want you to change the lessons you teach to the Acolytes. We are not going to teach Priest Robin's account anymore. Instead I will find a scroll to teach about people being brought together with parties, and stories that instill a sense of community."

"I will not teach your filthy lies. I will not teach the Acolytes to embrace shadow. As long as I'm Head Teacher they will be taught the real path of the Mission."

"And you're definitely sure of that," she said, raising her voice to make sure people heard.

Britta narrowed her eyes and pointed at her. "I will defend the faith with my life if I have to."

"Then I'm afraid I'm going to have to let you go as Head Teacher," she said, sadly. Despite the anger towards Britta she still felt sad that she was going to lose one of her closest friends. Why did it have to be like this? Why was Britta so stubborn?

Britta laughed and put up her hands. "You see faithful, you see how our shadow filled Keeper is firing me because of my views. You should all be worried about this. If you step out of line you will be next."

Sonja was a little bemused about that argument. Her mother had forced many faithful to quit because of their indiscretions or evidence of shadow. But apparently to Britta, it was her that was the tyrant.

"It has nothing to do with your views Britta. I accept that you have a different view than mine and I even accept your right to shout those views on my field. But teaching the Acolytes the right lessons is my job as the Keeper. Last night we had a very successful festival that brought people together. I want the Acolytes to learn a lesson from that, but you have told me you refuse to teach it. If you accept teaching it, I will keep you in your post."

But of course Britta never would teach it, and she said as much. "You are perverting the future of our children. Be aware people. If you find your faith collapsing around you, don't say I didn't warn you."

Britta gave Sonja one last sneer, turned around, and stomped off. Sonja watched her go. Her heart thumped, and she breathed like she had just ran from one end of the wagon train to another.

As she watched Britta disappear out of the encampment, the weight of sadness grew heavy. Why couldn't Britta accept her changes to the faith, why couldn't she accept that the festival last night had been a success, and why couldn't she accept someone loving the same sex as them? But Sonja knew she would never get any truly thought out answers from her. It would all just be what the texts said and how they needed to be pure. The words of their mother living on after death.

The faithful on the field had been trying to appear like they had not been eavesdropping on their loud conversation. They shook their heads at Britta, and some muttered good riddance. After Sonja joined back with them a few did say that she made the right choice in firing Britta.

Sonja breathed a sigh of relief. Her cleverness had paid off, and no one thought at the moment she was a tyrant. She basked in the glow of making another right decision, putting away the sadness of Britta leaving out of her mind. But it wasn't long until she had another worry to obsess over, and that was when to tell the faithful her secret.

YOU'RE ALWAYS IN THE SHADOW OF HEROES, ALWAYS TRYING TO MATCH AN OLD IDEAL THAT YOU NEVER TRULY CAN

'In The Shadow Of Heroes' by Katrina Caradog

It felt like the wagon train had perched upon the top of this hill forever. It had only been about a month, but with being named Jarl, finding out about Hannes' army, and participating in the harvest festival, it had felt like a whole lifetime to Sigrun. But things were coming to an end amongst the workers. They were displaying signs that it was time to move on. It wasn't that they wouldn't like to settle if they could, it was just they had gotten so used to traveling that it felt weird to be in one location for so long. It was time to figure out where the wagon train's next destination would be.

Usually this would be chosen solely by the Keeper, but Sonja was new to the role, Sigrun wanted to prove to the workers that she would make decisions, and they both wanted to foster union between the two sides, so the two of them decided to pick the destination together. However, before Sigrun talked to Sonja she wanted to understand the choices and what she would pick on her own.

Sigrun sat in the corner of her wagon, her desk covered with various detailed maps of the surrounding area. Her door was open. Bright red light streamed in, and a cool wind rustled her tunic, with the occasional sounds of people going about their day, horses trotting, and the gentle creak of the wagon wafting in.

She really should be outside, enjoying the late spring light, but instead she had to be squirreled away in her wagon picking out destinations. No one understood how the life of a Jarl was so hard sometimes.

There were a few paths on the map open to the wagon train: to the west there was the Glass Forest, they could follow the river north east to the city of Munn, or they could go south across the grass plain where they wouldn't meet any form of civilization for a few months until they hit the merchant cities on the coast.

None of the paths felt right. Her preference would be to go into the Glass Forest and find out about the ancient tribe that had constructed the glass. But that would mean having to go to Eik, which as the map - and Gregor and Yael -

indicated was a no go. Also she doubted that the wagon train as a whole would be as interested as her in knowing where the glass came from. Unfortunately, going across the plain would be risky, if their food or water ran low there would be no town or trade for miles. She guessed that left Munn, but what would they be going there for? They could pick up some extra food and have a few days of experiencing a new place, but that didn't feel like it would truly satisfy people.

So what would truly satisfy people? The only answer Sigrun could think of was to settle down somewhere.

Would the faith ever accept that? After all, it was their Mission to go out into the world and spread the message that Sol was going to appear in the sky again, but only if the people changed their ways for good. Sigrun didn't totally believe in that message but Sonja and the faithful did, and it was their wagon train as much as it was her people's. Would the faith ever abandon their Mission?

But then again it truly felt like Sonja was changing the faith. Sonja was much more focused on bringing the greater wagon train into the faithful's fold. The harvest festival was a great success when it came to that. Could Sigrun persuade her that the best way to bring the two sides together was to accept the workers' desire to stop traveling and to settle down.

It would be a hard sell, but Sigrun felt positive that she could be the one to sell it. The relationship she had with Sonja was excellent at the moment, she could say with all honesty that she loved Sonja. Sigrun knew Sonja to be the type of person to hear out her argument and see the bigger picture. She felt that she could convince Sonja that a unified wagon train in harmony with the faith of Sol was more reachable than trying to bring good to the whole world.

At the thought of the wagon train changing, Sigrun got a thrill. She gathered up her maps and put them under her arm. But when she turned around she found Sven standing in the doorway.

Sven didn't display any of his usual jolliness. Instead he had a hard stare, like the weight of the world had crashed onto him all of a sudden. Sigrun froze, frightened about what he was here for.

"My father wants to see you," Sven said, voice low.

He didn't say anymore, and Sigrun felt like

now wasn't a good time to question what it was about. Though she had a feeling it had to do with Gregor Baldur's illness. She put down her maps, and followed him out of the wagon.

The smell inside Gregor Baldur's wagon was horribly memorable for Sigrun. The same rotten smell had permeated her family's wagon when her mother had been sick. Back then they had tried to mask it with the smell of squeezed peaches or oranges, but the horrible smell still lingered. It was the same in Gregor's wagon, despite the smell of lavender and other strong flowers, every time she took a step down the long wagon the smell got more and more putrid.

    The sight of Gregor Baldur was similar to her mother as well. He had been thick armed and well built, but now he looked thin and tired, like he had aged thirty years in the time Sigrun had seen him last. He sat up in the bed, but it looked like it took all his effort to do so. His eyes were a little glassy, and every moment or so he grimaced in pain.

    Sigrun wanted to turn around and walk right out of the door. Everyday in her later childhood see her sick mother, those thin arms, that raspy voice, and that look of pain. Seeing Gregor like that made her see her mother in the same place, like a ghostly image. Like back then she didn't want to face up to the reality that Gregor was sick and was going to die.

But she wasn't here for her, she was here because he had requested it. And even though it frightened her to be here, she pushed out those feelings of running away. She stepped towards him. Gregor smiled weakly, and waved his son out of the wagon.

"As you can see the rumors about my health are true," he said, voice soft, so she had to lean closer to hear.

"You look absolutely fit to me, I can see you running around the wagon a few times," she said.

Gregor laughed at that, which turned into a cough. Sigrun felt a little guilty about that.

"My sons and nephews always said you were entertaining, I can see what they mean now," he said, struggling to straighten up more. "But come, sit, I've got something important to tell you."

She sat in the chair next to the bed. It felt warm, like someone had sat in it not too long ago. She guessed it had been Joan. She wondered how she was taking all of this. Sigrun's father had definitely not taken his wife's sickness very well, but Sigrun didn't see Joan as being the type to be away from home, drinking all day, and staggering back to sleep it off. Joan was made of sterner stuff.

"What did you want to tell me?" she asked.

"I am feeling the end, so I feel I need to get things off my chest and stop the lies I have told. Me and Yael didn't vote Hannes out of the Jarl position just because of the food problem, we also found out that he had been recruiting an army to go against the faith."

Sigrun tried to act like she hadn't known this information, but her acting ability must not have been great, because Gregor exclaimed, "You knew?"

"I may have discovered it while taking a night time stroll. I didn't say anything because I didn't know why you hadn't told me, and was worried about what would happen if you knew I knew."

Gregor grimaced, and shook his head. "You were the new Jarl, we should have told you, but we didn't know where your loyalties lied."

"My loyalty," she said, confused. "What do you mean?"

"You know for sometime now the three families

have drifted away from the faith - well the Mattsons were never with the faith, but you know what I mean. The old Keeper was way too strict on what she was allowing in the wagon, proselytizing her holier than thou attitude, and turning up her nose at us. Even our family, who have defended the faith through thick and thin, saw the tides turn. So when Jarl Matteus decided to abandon the wagon train to live in Tro, we had to decide on a new Jarl. And all three families decided on Hannes."

Gregor sighed, which turned into a hiss. "The reason we picked Hannes was to find some way to get rid of the faith's power." He weakly put up his hand, almost like he was expecting an objection. "Now this was meant to be peaceful, we just wanted to find some way to legally get us in power so we could decide what happened with the wagon train. But obviously Hannes pursued it in non-peaceful means."

"Rita Mattson obviously knew about the army stuff, but me and Yael hadn't. But I would have expected Yael to have let it go, if it wasn't for me who felt uncomfortable about it. I didn't want bloodshed against the faith. I didn't agree with what they had become, but they were still, in a sense, family. Hell some of my nephews are married to the Priestesses. Killing them would be killing our own. So I brought in the vote against Hannes, begging Yael to follow suit. It was only after I revealed that I was dying that he agreed, as a gift for me."

"This doesn't explain why you had to hide it from the council, or from me," Sigrun said.

"We didn't tell the faith because Hannes was our creation. If we told the faith they would have known that we brought him in for the sole purpose of getting rid of them. The Keeper would have punished the whole wagon train for that, we'd be under her purity tyranny forever. And we didn't tell you because we didn't know whether you would tell the faith. You were an unknown, so we didn't know where your loyalties lied."

"So why are you telling me now?"

"Because we were completely wrong," he said, coughing. "Me and Yael were completely wrong to doubt you, and we were completely wrong to bring in Hannes. From what I've heard this new Keeper is making the effort to bring the people together again. She is getting rid of the whole purity drive, and wanting to connect with us."

He slapped his hands hard on the cover. "But Hannes is still building up his army. He is still waiting for the chance to rise up. I wanted to tell you because I wanted to warn you, but it looks like you were already warned. But it's still good to get it off my chest, to tell you the true reason why we didn't tell you. It was a bad reason, but there you are."

Sigrun sat in the chair, absorbing everything Gregor had just said. It all felt like political maneuvering to her, something she didn't really understand. Why couldn't they just live with the faith in peace? Why did they have to jostle with them for supremacy and power? It truly felt like this wagon train was divided right in the middle.

In fact it was divided even more than two: the Mattsons and the Hoademakers looked onto the Baldurs with envy and wanted to be in a similar position in terms of power, and the Hoademakers and Matssons looked at each other, fighting it out to be more powerful than the other. All these people with their power plays didn't care about what to do with that power, whether that power should be used to help people. It was just used to enrich themselves.

Did she really have to play in that game as well? She didn't want to, she just wanted to do what the people wanted.

Gregor leant over to her, grimacing as he put out his hands. "Can you ever forgive me?"

She hated that Gregor had brought Hannes in, had some ties with the army he was gathering, and hadn't told her about any of it. She wanted to be angry. But then she looked at him: his frail body, his tired eyes, his deathly cough, that rotten smell, and couldn't be. What was the harm in forgiving this man who was soon going to die?

"I forgive you," she said, grabbing hold of his hand and squeezing.

Gregor's smile, for a brief moment, seemed to transform him into his younger and stronger self. It felt good to give someone that smile. But then the weakness and the illness took over again, and Gregor slumped back into bed.

Sigrun stood up in the chair, patted his hand again, and walked down the wagon. While she did, Gregor's frail body in her mind seemed to merge into her mother's body again. When she opened the door, tears streamed down her cheeks.

***

On Sonja's way through Bonde Square she passed Sigrun, but there were no waves or smiles. Sigrun looked upset. There was a part of Sonja that wanted to follow her and ask what was wrong. She didn't like to see Sigrun upset like that, but it felt like the visit to Gregor was more important at the moment. So all Sonja could do was stare at Sigrun as she went past, and tell herself that she would visit her after seeing Gregor.

It had been a surprise to hear that Gregor wanted to see her. All she remembered of the big man were the visits with her mother. Most of these visits were when she was a child, so she only saw him step into the Keeper's wagon and after a few hours step out again. But these visits soon stopped when she was a teenager. The last time Gregor visited Sonja's mother, he had stomped out of her mother's wagon and shouted how she was going against the farmers and how he couldn't accept her new purity path.

Before that the Baldurs were always an important family to the faith. They always came to morning and evening prayers. Their sons, nephews, and workers mixed socially with Priests and Priestesses and sometimes even married them. The Baldurs had always defended them when other families attacked their ways, and would usually vote for their laws within the council. After that meeting it all ceased, except for the occasional get together and marriage.

With all that bad blood between the faith and the Baldurs, Sonja wondered why she had been personally summoned.

It wasn't hard to understand when she saw Gregor in his bed, and smelled the rottenness of his room. She was shocked to see how weak and tired he looked. The black beard had turned gray and scraggly, and none of the braids were tied up. There were dark rings around his eyes, and a gauntness to his face. Seeing it made Sonja have to close her eyes, breathe deeply, and push herself forwards. It was clear Gregor was going to die soon.

She strode over to him, making herself display a serene smile - even though she was absolutely heartbroken and terrified to see a big man brought so low - and bowed. "It is an honor to be called in by the eminent Gregor Baldur. How may I serve?"

Gregor waved the compliment away, coughing in the process. Sonja could see small bits of blood on the pillow.

"You don't have to prop me up as more than I am," he said, voice like a croaky whisper. "I know there has been some distance between me and the faith."

"But there is always time to bring us closer together again," she said, walking over to his side and squeezing his hand.

Gregor examined her. "You really do want to bring the two sides of the wagon train together, don't you?"

"Very much so, it's a travesty to our very Mission that our neighbors hate us. How can we convert others when we cannot even convert the ones closest to us, have made them drift away from us even," she said, sitting down in the chair.

"I was skeptical that the faith could change," Gregor said. "But hearing what happened at the festival, and seeing you, I am no longer worried. You're doing a great job at trying to get rid of the problems your mother caused."

Sonja nodded, remembering the portrait of her mother showing her as passionate. "One thing my mother was strong at was pursuing things and making them real. It is unfortunate that she pursued the wrong things."

"Even when you are changing these things, it still surprises me to hear you call them wrong," Gregor said. "Do you not feel…close to what your mother did? Do you not feel some kind of guilt for going against her ways so deliberately?"

"No, because my mother's ways hurt me more than your farmers'. I was made to feel shame about who I am." Sonja shook her head. "But this isn't about me, this is about you."

Gregor looked down at the bed, seemingly ashamed. It was a surprise to her that this giant leader would feel something like that.

"I wanted to tell you my shadow, in the hope that I could go to Sol with only light inside," he said.

"And what is your shadow?" she asked.

"I have sowed the seeds of the faith's destruction."

And he told her about Hannes. How the Elders of three families voted him in as Jarl in order to take away the faith's power. How Hannes had taken that goal to mean building up an army to violently get rid of the faith. Even though Sonja knew some of this from what Sigrun had told her, it still felt like a blow to hear it out loud, to have someone like Gregor try to excuse it while also understanding he was guilty. When the explanation was over, both her and Gregor fell silent.

The silence was heavy and awkward, only broken up by Gregor coughing. Eventually he sighed, and stared at her. "Do you think Sol will forgive me?"

She didn't know whether she could forgive him, but looking at him now, at his weak body, at the knowledge that he was going to die soon, she felt that it would be cruel not to give him what he wanted.

"I think she can, if you acknowledge your shadows, and make sure to counteract the deeds with light," she said.

Gregor's face lit up, looking for a brief moment like he was thirty years younger. "I will insist to Sven to vote in this new law of Sigrun's, to try to stem Hannes recruitment. I will also make sure my son, and the farmers, help you in your endeavors to unify the wagon train. I feel doing this will cast a light big enough to counteract my shadows."

She leant forwards, and squeezed his hand. "I do believe it will."

Gregor's eyes filled up with tears, and he squeezed her hand back. "Thank you so much."

Sonja stood up. "I believe I should pray with you, and prepare you for your journey to Sol, whenever that happens."

"I feel it's going to happen soon," he said, wiping his eyes.

The two of them closed their eyes, and said prayers to Sol. Sonja prayed for his shadows to be banished, and for him to be shown the light of Sol, and when he died for him to be taken to where Sol resided. Gregor finished off the prayer by praying for the wagon train to become unified, for Sonja's plan to be enacted fully, and for the future to be filled with as much light as possible.

In that moment she felt the closest she had ever been to a proper Keeper. When she had been named Keeper she felt like an impostor in the job, feeling like she didn't have the grace or authority for it. Every time she met people as the Keeper it felt like an act that was going to be found out at any moment. But now, fulfilling what Gregor wanted from her and praying to Sol, she felt like she was meant for this job. She could change the faith to something positive, all she had to do was try.

When Sonja ended the prayers, she was thankful to Gregor for allowing her to finally be confident in the role as the Keeper. Even though he had brought in Hannes, and had some hand with bringing in the army that wanted to destroy the faith, she still felt sad that he was going to pass on from this world. She felt that the wagon train would be worse off without him in it.

She walked out of the wagon. Tears streamed down her cheeks.

> TO SEE THE MONSTERS THAT HAUNTED YOU AT NIGHT IN THE COLD LIGHT OF DAY IS ALWAYS COMICAL. A FEROCIOUS BEAST STALKING YOUR DOOR BECOMES NOTHING BUT AN OLD COAT
>
> *'Fearsome Shadows Of A Mouse' by Mohini Hagir*

Sigrun walked back to her wagon, feeling a terrible weight inside. Images flashed in her mind of her mother's weak body, her raspy voice, and the final closing of her eyes. Sigrun tried to push the images out of her mind, saying to herself that it was long ago and she couldn't do anything about it now. But that didn't stop the images from coming.

The only thing that could cure her dull pain was to get into bed and read a fable from her mother's book. That would make her feel a little better. By reading them she would be transported to a time when her mother was alive and full of power, not when she was weak and vulnerable.

But she wouldn't get her wish, as an unlikely person stood at her wagon door. Hannes leant against the wagon, arms folded. Seeing his swept back blond hair and grin caused Sigrun to sigh.

She really wasn't in the mood for this.

"I never thought I'd get to see my predecessor," she said, as strong as she could manage.

"I've been around the Mattsons, I'm sure you could have found me if you wanted," he said, straightening up and putting out his hand.

Sigrun looked down, ignored it, and opened the door. "I feel it's always good to try to ignore those who have come before you, find your own path."

"But there are so many mistakes that we can steer you from," Hannes said, clearly not taking the hint that he should go away.

"I've heard about your mistakes. I feel I can avoid them quite easily."

Hannes didn't stop smiling, and his hand was still out wanting her to shake it. "I feel we should talk."

She sighed again, feeling that the only way that she was going to get rid of him was to hear what he had to say, so she opened the door and waved him in.

When Hannes saw the rough wood with splinters poking out of them, the askew shelf, the wardrobe that wouldn't shut, and the general mess, he looked confused.

"Did Yael and Gregor not give you the Jarl's

wagon?" he asked, like he was offended on her behalf.

Sigrun couldn't help but smile. He had no clue what she was like or what she preferred. He assumed that Yael and Gregor had given her a bum deal and that he would come in to save her. Little did he know that this daggy wagon was where she felt perfectly comfortable. And if he didn't know what she really was like he was coming into this meeting with bad grounding.

"They gave me the Jarl's wagon, but I decided it just wasn't for me," she said, as innocently as possible.

Hannes looked surprised at this, but then he went back to grinning. "Ah, a way of showing the people that you are one of them. I'm surprised I didn't think of that."

Of course, everything to Hannes was a political game. To him there was no genuine action or belief, everything a Jarl did was a calculation to gain the most power or popularity. It felt sad that this was the Jarl before her. How could the people accept someone that seemed so fake?

She sat on the bed, and gestured for Hannes to sit in the chair at the desk. "What do I owe the pleasure, then?"

Hannes leaned forward, lowering his voice like he was about to whisper a conspiracy. "I know about the law you're bringing in about reducing parties. I'm here to tell you that's a very bad idea. You've done well to get people on your side, but this law will set them against you. You may think the faith is giving you no choice, they feel strong so I can understand the pressure, but you can go against them. You'll be safe if you do."

Sigrun had to stop herself from laughing. Hannes thought that she was a little lost lamb in this job, only doing what the grown ups told her to do. It would be insulting if it wasn't just a little bit funny. And she had been worried about this guy, his political influence, his army? Seeing him sprouting this nonsense made them all feel like ghosts that disappear when you shine a light on them.

"And what protection would that be? What would I get if I didn't vote in this law?" she asked, wanting him to admit his secrets.

"I don't want to say too much," he said, looking around the wagon. "But the faith won't be the only force in this place for too long. And as for the benefits for going down my route, well you'll be the Keeper of my parties. Every time I make one your name will come up, hell you could be a VIP if you want to be. It'll give you a good in with the people you want to lead, and will allow you to be on the ground level of the future of the wagon train."

"The ground level of the future of the wagon train, you talk in such grand terms but don't give me any specifics," she said.

But Hannes was too clever to be led into her trap. He just shrugged, and said, "It's dangerous to go into specifics sometimes. You never know what side people are on, and I was just voted out of my job."

"So tell me, what would happen if I didn't go with your plan. What mistake would I be making?"

"Oh, a big one. The people love my weekly parties, it's the lifeblood of this wagon train. No where else do they get a chance just to forget their work and their plight."

"And what plight would that be?" she asked.

Hannes gave her a hard stare. "Being forced to follow a faith they do not believe in."

Sigrun shook her head. "You must have not attended the harvest festival. The faith has changed, and people's attitude towards them have changed as well. The faith wants to unify the wagon train, bringing both sides together. A few days ago I talked with the people and they told me they felt positively about the faith."

"Ah but something can always happen to dampen that enthusiasm," Hannes said, wiping her desk with his hand. "The faith and the people of the wagon train have divergent goals. They will eventually come into conflict, like maybe the people will want to settle down. The faith will never accept that, it goes against their Mission."

Sigrun felt a little chill from that. Was he right, would the faith ever accept that proposal? But she dismissed the worry. She had something that Hannes never had, a great relationship with the woman who ran the faith.

"I disagree," she said, feeling more sure of herself. "What did you say earlier, yes that was it, I feel the relationship between the people and the faith now is the ground level of the future of the wagon train. These laws I am creating are a part of that. No longer will people worry about starvation because the food has been wasted on parties, no longer will the sweat of the farmers' labor be thrown away just because people want to forget their troubles. Instead, they will think positively about their fellow caravaners because they will talk with them and become friendly with them at these designated celebrations."

Hannes sighed. "As I said, you're making a big mistake."

"And will you make it a mistake?" she said, as icily as possible.

Hannes laughed, and pushed himself off the chair. "You have no idea who you are dealing with. You're clever, I give you that, but I have the weight of the families on my side. I hope you enjoy your power as long as it lasts. But know that the ground of the future I talked about will be laid, no matter how many dead bodies we have to bury under it."

He smiled an evil smile, and walked out the door.

When he was gone, Sigrun burst out laughing. All of Hannes' posture and threats felt so weak. He was clearly scared of the party's law, and had visited to persuade her to stop it. All it felt like was empty threats. It made her feel that his power was going to collapse soon, and she was going to collapse it.

She chuckled, as she took *'How Manang Ate The Sun, and Other Fables'* down from the shelf.

Sigrun crawled into bed, pulling the covers up to her chin. She had nothing to worry about.

THE OTHER LOVER SAID STEP ON BOARD. BUT THERE WAS A LARGE RIVER BETWEEN THEM

'Two Lovers Meet' Skald Song

Sonja knocked on Sigrun's door. She looked around, noticing a few people milling about or sitting down at tables near their wagons. The faith encampment just across the grass was filled with Priests, Priestesses, and Acolytes gathering together in groups and chatting away. Sonja would not be able to stay long, which disappointed her.

When Sigrun opened her door, her eyes looked blurry, and there was red down her cheeks. She must have been crying after her visit with Gregor. Not a surprise as the whole situation had been very emotional and sad. However, Sigrun did manage a smile when she saw her, and waved her in.

When the world had been shut out, they hugged. The feeling of Sigrun in her arms brought warmth and strength back to her. She caressed Sigrun's back, and kissed her.

"I just wanted to see if you were ok," she said.

Sigrun put her head onto her shoulder. "I think I'm ok."

They stood in each other's arms. For how long, Sonja didn't know, but each moment in that embrace felt glorious and right. She could have stayed in that embrace forever, but eventually Sigrun broke away.

"You probably want to catch up, but I feel we need to discuss something important," Sigrun said, walking over to the desk in the corner.

The desk was strewn with papers messily laid about. When Sonja looked closer she could see they were maps.

Sigrun unrolled one of them, and gestured for her to see. "The harvest is over so we are going to have to pick a destination to head off to. I thought we should decide together."

Sonja smiled. It felt like a big moment for them to be deciding something for the wagon train together. Not only were they connecting on a personal level but they were also connecting as leaders. Sonja felt her heart beat fast. Would her vision about being in union together, and thus bringing the wagon train together, turn out to be true? This felt like an important step on that journey.

The two of them stood side by side at the desk. Each time Sigrun moved her arm it brushed up against Sonja's. Every touch was a little thrill to her. She hated the fact that she couldn't grab Sigrun right now, kiss her passionately, and pull her onto the bed. That thought made her neck and head heat up, and she had to step away a little from Sigrun and shake her head a little to cool off.

Sigrun pointed at the map, which showed the hill, river, and Glass Forest, in some detail. "So there are a few paths we can take: follow the river towards Munn, go through the Glass Forest and pass Eik, or go across the grass plains and hope we make it to the merchants without starving to death."

"It intrigues me that you don't say go to Eik, and I see there is a big cross next to it on the map," she said.

Sigrun laughed. "That's because Eik doesn't like the faith that much. If we choose there I will have a lot of the leaders shouting at me about it being a bad choice."

"So the most logical choice then is Munn."

"I don't think we should choose any of the paths," Sigrun said, picking up another map, this time of the Glass Forest. "There is a spot to the north, near some hills, where a river flows out. It's on the border between the Glass Forest and a small area of grass. I think we should go there and settle."

Sonja was confused. "What do you mean settle? We have already settled for our harvest. We won't do another for at most six months."

Sigrun closed her eyes, breathed in, opened them again. "I mean settle permanently. I think the wagon train should find a good bit of land, which this is, and stay there."

"Don't be ridiculous, that goes against what we are, what our Mission is."

"I thought you were changing the Mission, bringing us closer together."

"Yes, I want to bring the wagon train closer together," Sonja said, shocked that they were even discussing this. "But that's because it feels wrong to go out there to proselytize when we haven't even brought on board our neighbors."

"Well, there you go, you'll have plenty of time to bring the people over if we are in one place," Sigrun said, smiling.

Did Sigrun not understand? It confused her that she was saying this with all sincerity and belief. "The whole point of getting the people on board is for them to join us on our Mission. The Mission is still the same. We still need to go out into the world and help it be good so Sol can return to the sky. Just what I feel is good has changed, we need to bring people together and fight the tyranny they face."

Sigrun stepped towards her, took her hand. "I don't want to tell you this, but the people aren't enthused about your Mission as the faith is. All they want to do is settle down in their own land, raise families, and live a good life. I've talked with them, they are sick of traveling."

"But that is why we will teach them our Mission, and get them to be enthusiastic about it. If we do it right we can come together on a journey that will fulfill their hearts."

"It's too late," Sigrun said, softly. "The divide has already happened. A few months ago they went so far as to vote someone in as Jarl that stated to build an army to get rid of you. This is what the people want."

Sonja pulled her hand away from her. "I will not give up on our Mission. You may not understand it, but it is the most important thing in my life. Without that we are nothing, we will do nothing. Living our lives happily is not enough, the world out there is an icy wasteland. We have the potential to change that."

"And what would you do if the people decided to rise up to get what they wanted?"

"Is that a threat?"

Sigrun looked annoyed. "How could you think I would threaten you?"

"I don't know, but what came out sounded like one."

"I'm just saying what's true. The people want to settle down and they are frustrated that their wishes aren't being heard. When people get frustrated enough they start breaking things," Sigrun said, pacing up and down. "Think about it, you could be the most popular Keeper in our history if you gave them what they wanted. You would have everyone here praising Sol."

"We need the world to praise Sol if we are going to save it," Sonja said.

"Do you not see how ridiculous that goal is? It will never happen. How many centuries have your faith gone out there to proselytize your message? How many towns or cities have you converted? Has it made any difference to the world?"

Sonja shook her head. She couldn't believe that she had fallen in love with someone that didn't get her or her faith. It wasn't about whether they would make a difference in her lifetime, that was vanity speaking, it was about getting the small snowball to roll down the hill until it became so big it could change the world around it.

"This wagon train was founded on our Mission, and it is that Mission we are going to pursue."

"So you are going to keep the people prisoner?" Sigrun asked, disgusted.

"They joined this wagon train by their own choice, they knew what it was, what it was about. Now they complain when it isn't what they wanted. If they felt so badly they would get off at the next town."

Sigrun shook her head. "It was their great, great, great grandparents that chose to be in this wagon train, not them. Their families, friends, and homes are here, and they don't want to lose them."

"Well then, they'll just have to get used to a life on the road all the time and stop complaining about it."

Sigrun was probably about to say some more, but Sonja had heard enough. The excitement she felt at the start, feeling like they would come together to make a decision had disappeared. Now

Sonja felt angry, hurt, and sad all at the same time.

How could Sigrun be so obsdinate and not give her path a chance? How could she be so dismissive of what she believed? What had happened to the person that seemed to get her. Had she been truly there?

She opened up the wagon door, feeling hot. Every step outside made the buzz of anger dissipate, turning into a weight of sadness. What did this fight with Sigrun mean for their relationship? What did it mean for her dream of unifying the wagon train? She didn't totally know, but she did feel the answer wouldn't be a good one.

WE PRAY TO LEAD YOUR SOUL INTO THE SKY, AND SO YOU MAY FIND THE HIDDEN RESTING PLACE OF SOL

Mission Of Sol Funeral Prayer

Sigrun didn't see Sonja after the argument. At the start it was mainly because she didn't want to see her, still angry at the fact that she had dismissed what she had said out of hand. How could Sonja not see that the people wanted something different from their lives than following the Mission? It felt like Sonja just didn't want to see the truth and would pursue what the faith wanted no matter whether the people of the wagon train wanted that.

Eventually that anger subsided, and Sigrun began to wonder whether she shared some of the blame for the argument. Could she have been stubborn herself? Could she have tried to understand Sonja's arguments more instead of being offended they weren't what she wanted?

As the days went on Sigrun understood that she probably could have listened and discussed things with Sonja more. This realization led her to slap herself on the forehead. How could she be so stupid? She stroked her braid and worried that she had completely messed up their relationship.

After that she avoided Sonja deliberately. She didn't want to see any evidence that Sonja was still mad at her, that she still felt hurt by what she had done. Sigrun didn't know what she would do if Sonja didn't want to be with her, even just thinking about that plunged a dagger in her heart and made her cry.

To distract herself, she dedicated her time to doing her Jarl duties. This meant going out into the wider wagon train, inspecting wagons and testing them to see if they moved when prompted, talking to people and checking to see if they were ok, and exploring the different streets and squares.

Since she felt she had spent too much time in Bonde Square with the farmers, she paid a visit to the Hoademakers and the Mattsons.

The Hoademakers were more accommodating to her. They all lived in finely made wagons and dressed in great tailored tunics and cloaks. Sigrun couldn't deny that she felt a little dirty and grubby in comparison, but she kept reminding herself that the muddy tunic and disheveled look was who she was. She talked to the important family members about her new law limiting parties and why it needed to be brought in. The Hoademakers seemed to understand, but they had concerns about whether the other families would agree and what the tension would do to the wider wagon train. She told them that the law seemed to be popular with the farmers, which changed their tune to one of positivity.

At the end of her visit, she got the impression that the Hoedemakers calculated things a little too much when it came to politics. They always wanted to be on a neutral footing with everyone, and not be seen to rock the wagon. It never felt like they really had any ambitions or dreams of their own, they just wanted to keep the power they had already.

The Mattsons were the complete opposite. They definitely had their own ideas of how they wanted things to be run, and they didn't mind telling Sigrun about them. When she walked through Mattson Square she got a lot of dirty looks from every man or woman that sat at the sides. Some shouted how she was ruining the wagon train by getting rid of the weekly parties, others shouted how Hannes shouldn't have been voted out. She tried to explain why she was getting rid of the parties, telling them that it was a waste of food and that there was always the worry of starvation. But the Mattsons dismissed the concern, saying that they could trade for food or the farmers could grow more. Sigrun tried to get an audience with Rita Mattson, hoping that she could be persuaded to vote for the new laws, but the guards outside her wagon said she was busy.

Feeling defeated, Sigrun walked around the Mattsons' streets, smelling the cooked food from the kitchen wagons, watching the groups of men and women hang around and chat to each other. Unfortunately, she couldn't do this for long as some of them shouted at her, or strode up and threatened her. Not wanting to start a fight with the whole family, she exited the encampment.

The rest of her days were spent in her wagon, talking to workers who came to her with problems with the party law. The workers told her they liked the parties because it allowed them to relax and forget about work. She reiterated her promise of giving them a whole day where they could relax and not work. They liked this idea, but replied with how the parties allowed them to be social with their friends and have a good time. She saw their point and said that maybe they could create informal gatherings and parties, but that they could not use any food. When she said this the workers seemed satisfied.

An important Baldur came around to talk to her about this day off she was promising. It wasn't Sven, but some younger cousin who had curly black hair and a small nose. He asked how the day off was going to work, and she told him that it would be like the lunch or after harvest breaks just for a whole entire day. He worried about productivity, but she told him having some kind of rest might raise productivity, as his workers wouldn't be constantly tired. He seemed to be leaning towards favorability, but then said that some work like planting of the crops or harvesting did have to be an everyday thing otherwise they could ruin crops. She said she would look into that and have a meeting with the Baldurs and the farmers so they could come to some sort of arrangement for those times.

"Of course, the wagon train does need to head off soon," the young Baldur said. "We have probably been here longer than necessary."

Sigrun sighed. She would have to talk to Sonja about that, and they would have to decide something. They could just ignore the argument they had last time and just pick a destination, but she felt that was pushing the problem further down the road. Eventually they would have to talk about the future of the wagon train, and since everything was positive with the people and her new law – well except for Hannes, but he would soon lose his power – now was a good time to have the conversation. But could they have it without arguing again? Was there no solution they could come to?

The problem was the two sides were so diametrically opposed. One wanted to stay and the other wanted to go, how could you ever find a compromise to that? But she felt they had to, not just for the unity of the wagon rain but also for the unity of their relationship.

She decided that on the next day she would go to Sonja and they would discuss the problem like adults. She would stop herself from taking it so personally and hear out Sonja's side of things. Hopefully they could be mature enough to decide something without breaking up.

Unfortunately the next day Gregor Baldur died.

The next time Sigrun saw Sonja was at the funeral. But Sonja carried out the ceremony in the middle of Bonde Square, while Sigrun stood with the crowd of farmers on the sidelines. All Sigrun could do was stare at Sonja, wanting the hours to go by quickly so they could actually talk.

Sonja held a long silver chain with an incense holder at the end. She walked around a pyre that looked like the lower half of a wagon, with flowers arranged on top. Gregor slept in the middle. While Sonja walked around the pyre she waved the incense, wafting a white cloud into the air, smelling like cinnamon and apples.

"We all pray to lead your soul into the sky," Sonja shouted.

Priests, Priestesses, and prominent Baldurs – including Sven – all bowed their heads and echoed the words.

Sigrun tried to keep her mind on Gregor, tried to think about him and what he meant to her and the wagon train, but her mind kept coming back to Sonja. She should have been grateful for Gregor naming her Jarl, or sad that he was gone, but she hadn't really known him that much. It just felt like her and Sonja's relationship getting back on track was much more important than being at this funeral.

But she knew how it would look if she didn't seem mournful and upset, so she faked a sad expression and muttered the faithful's prayers like everyone else.

Unfortunately, the funeral took a couple of hours. Sonja and the faithful walked around the pyre waving incense, prayers were muttered to lead Gregor towards Sol, and his wife, sons, nephews, and other important Baldurs recited stories about Gregor or talked about how much he meant to them. At the end, Sven walked up to the pyre with a lit torch and set the flowers, the half wagon, and Gregor's body on fire, while everyone muttered the final prayer.

Even after the funeral, Sigrun couldn't find a chance to talk to Sonja. She was never alone, always talking with one of the Baldurs or Joan, and the conversation always sounded like they were discussing Gregor's life. It wasn't the type of conversation that you could barge in and say, "Hey Sonja, can we talk about our argument a few days ago?"

Instead she sampled the beer barrels around the square, and milled about with the farmers and the funeral goers. She naturally found herself in the group that contained Thore, Daniel, and Aina. They were all looking solemn and talking about how Gregor's death was the end of an era.

"He was the one who truly knew the struggles

of the wagon train." Thore said, sipping his mead. "I heard that Sven never really wanted to listen to him, just wanted to play lords with his friends."

Aina shook her head. "We should never forget the struggles we have had against the faith."

Sigrun furrowed her brows, the funeral they had just attended was all about the faith. "I thought the farmers were ok with the faith now? The harvest festival they threw was good."

Daniel spat on the ground. "Takes more than a harvest festival to make up for their past tyranny."

Thore narrowed his eyes. "Yeah, and we know that you want to help them with your new party law."

"I'm not helping them, I'm helping you," she said, surprised this was coming from them. She thought they had been ok with the laws she had been proposing. "I don't want all your hard work going to waste."

"If it's our hard work, maybe we should have a say where it goes. And I say it goes on partying," Thore said, with nods of agreement from Daniel and Aina. "Your law sounds too much like banning parties to me, something only the faith wants to do."

"Where have you been getting that idea?" she asked.

They didn't answer, just shook their heads and ignored her. But it didn't take a lot of working out to know where they got it from: Hannes. After all, this group had been the one she followed to his secret army. It worried her that he had been able to turn them back to hating the law, but it was too late now and it felt like a lot of other farmers were behind the new law. Hopefully it would pass through the Council and take down Hannes once and for all, which would mean he wouldn't be able to poison the minds of any more people about the faith. Then this group would be able to appreciate the law again.

She shook her head, and left the group. She looked around the square at all the people in their various different groups. Even though she was their leader and she felt personable towards them, she felt at that moment like a lost calf. Everyone had people that they were telling stories to, or crying with, or laughing alongside, everyone except her. She stood on the grass in the square alone. There was no one she knew here that she could tell stories to, cry with, or laugh alongside. Except Sonja.

Sigrun walked towards her flame robes, hoping that she would be alone. But swept back blond hair caught the corner of her eye. She looked, and at the edge of the square she could see Hannes. Curiously enough, he was talking to the curly haired woman that had kept protesting in the middle of the harvest festival. You usually didn't see a member of the faith talking with someone who hated the faith, so she snuck up to where they stood, in order to hear what they were saying.

"Is everything set?" the curly haired woman said.

"Yes, my people are in place," Hannes said, leaning towards the woman. "When they go in, my people will move the wagon and that's when we storm in."

"Do you think they'll really do it?"

"I think a group of people holding swords is very persuasive."

"As long as the Keeper steps down, that's what I ask," the curly haired woman said, harshly.

"After we get what we want, I promise," Hannes said.

Sigrun had no idea what they were planning but it didn't sound good. It sounded like Sonja was in danger. She had to warn her.

She rushed into the square, peering around for Sonja. She found her near Gregor's wagon, talking with Sven and a few other important Baldurs. Sigrun didn't care if she was barging into something sensitive, this was more important.

"Sonja, I have to speak to you."

Sonja narrowed her eyes, and glanced guiltily at the Baldurs. "Sigrun, this is an inappropriate time. Can you wait until after the funeral?"

"No, your life is in danger."

"What do you mean?"

"Please, can we speak in private?"

Sigrun didn't know why, but she didn't want to tell the Baldurs what she overheard with Hannes. There was still an element of distrust when it came to Sven and what he truly wanted. She knew Gregor wanted to go against Hannes, but did that extend to the rest of his family?

Sonja glanced towards the Baldurs. "Sorry about this."

They nodded and said they understood, however their faces showed that they were a little insulted about a mad Sigrun disrupting their chat.

"If this is a way for me to forgive you, I can tell you now it'll backfire," Sonja said, annoyed.

Sigrun shook her head. "It's not about us."

She told her what she had overheard Hannes and the Priestess say. Sonja looked visibly shocked by the end.

"Britta is really going to violently go against me? I can't believe it has gotten that far...we used to be friends," she muttered.

Sigrun grabbed Sonja's shoulders. "I don't know what they're planning but I want you to be safe. Get any weapon you can and have it on you at all times, but keep it concealed. I will keep an eye out, but without more details all we can do is react when it finally happens."

Sonja shook her head, clearly not able to process the severity of what was going on. She looked into Sigrun's eyes. "Have I done a good job as Keeper?"

"You've done a brilliant job. These people are just violent extremists that will never listen to reason. I've been trying to stop them with this party law, but they still have an army with swords, they can do some damage if they wanted to."

"Maybe I should get some bodyguards."

"That sounds like a good idea."

The two of them stood next to each other,

silent and a little awkward. Sigrun's heart pumped, and her brain buzzed. She slowly noticed that she was still holding onto Sonja's shoulders, and they were alone together. A dirty thought flashed in her mind, but she dismissed it. Then she thought this was the perfect time to try to speak to her about the wagon train's destination, but that decision felt so unurgent now. Eventually she just decided to take her hands off Sonja's shoulders.

"I don't want anything bad to happen to you," she said, sounding a little lame.

"Do you truly feel that, after the argument we had?"

"It was my fault, I was being too bullheaded and didn't think about what you were really saying."

Sonja laughed. "No it was my fault, I was the one that was stubborn and didn't think about what you were saying. I was just following the path I have been all my life, not really thinking whether anyone else wanted to go on it."

"Do you forgive me for my stupidity?"

"Do you forgive me for mine?"

"Shall we just say we were both stupid and forgive each other," Sigrun said, laughing.

"That sounds like a good plan."

They both hugged, which turned into a passionate kiss. Sigrun's heart leapt for joy, she hadn't completely fucked up her relationship with Sonja. The two of them could come together again, even after a fight.

This gave her some hope that the wider wagon train could come together as well. Sure, Hannes and Britta were going to try to attack that, but as long as her and Sonja were together they could take that on. And like she had said, they were extremists that wouldn't listen. Not everyone thought like them.

IT WAS IN THE MIDDLE OF SPRING WHEN HANNES ATTACKED

'The History Of The Wagon Train Vol. 8' by Jarl Sigrun

Sonja fished out a long knife from the faith's weapon storage and wrapped it around her leg. If Hannes or Britta decided to attack she would be ready. To protect herself further she searched around for Priests and Priestesses that looked hardy and strong and picked them to be her bodyguards. Two of them would stand outside her wagon, or flank her when she went out walking, and two of them would be patrolling the faith encampment or wider wagon train, and would report anything suspicious they found.

The first few days after being warned by Sigrun that an attack was imminent, Sonja's paranoia ate at her. She still had duties to do as a Keeper, and she had to search and interview faithful to find a new replacement for Britta as Head Teacher. But every time she sat down in a wagon to interview a candidate, or chatted to a faithful outside, she glanced behind or kept her gaze on the shadowy corners, imagining Hannes or Britta standing there ready to pounce. It was hard to sleep, as she stared at her bedroom door, hearing out for any creak of wood or any sound of metal. She was so on edge that she didn't really hear the answers from the people she interviewed, instead imagining any numerous ways that she could die.

However nothing actually happened. There was no attack by Hannes or Britta, no suspicious reports by her bodyguards, and no Priest or Priestess harbored any ill will to her.

On the contrary most in the faith encampment seemed to love her as their Keeper. Many faithful kept asking when the next get-together like the harvest festival was going to happen. She told them that they would need to vote for the new party law first, which was going to happen at the end of that week, and she would then sit down with Sigrun to determine on what dates throughout the year they would be held. She also needed to sit down with Sigrun to decide on the future of the wagon train, but she put that out of her mind. The thought of that argument made her anxious, as she didn't want a repeat of the break they had last time.

Eventually Sonja's extreme paranoia subsided to a more minor version. It was only as bad as checking the edges of the faith encampment while she was outside and occasionally glancing behind her during an interview.

In those interviews she started to pay attention more. A lot of the candidates that put themselves forwards only knew some of the scrolls by memory, so they were the first to go. Of the candidates that did know a lot of the scrolls, the question she posed to them was how much their teachings would be based on the actual text of the scrolls or someone else's interpretation.

Sonja felt that the best Head Teacher would teach the scrolls as they were written instead of teaching a specific message they saw in the text. Even though it would be good for her to push her community message further by insisting the Head Teacher taught it, she felt that would just be repeating the same mistakes as her mother in demanding a specific way of being faithful. For the faith to grow they had to be ok with different messages and opinions about the text. Sonja was confident that this wouldn't cause a fracture in the faith. The texts always had unambiguous messages about the truth of Sol coming back into the sky, the things they had to do to bring that about, and the importance of being unified as a community.

After many interviews with different Priests and Priestesses, Sonja decided that the best candidate was a woman named Hildegard. She had a bookish look, and seemed quite shy when talking to Sonja, but when questions about the scrolls came up she became passionate about their content. Her knowledge of the different stories and ideas within the scrolls was impressive, and Hildegard seemed fascinated by what the different sections would mean in terms of their message and what the faith should take away from them, but she never reduced that message to one particular rule that the faithful should follow.

Sure, Hildegard might need to gain some confidence if she was going to teach in front of children, but that could be gained. Sonja felt in every way that Hildegard was perfect for the job.

But the new Head Teachers first action was not going to be teaching the Acolytes. Instead it was going to be voting for Sigrun's party law.

Sven came over to the faith encampment and told them that it was time for the Council to sit. Some of Sven's old jolliness had come back, as he was smiling when he strode up towards Sonja, but his eyes still had some sadness.

Sonja gathered Roose, Teresa, Sigmund, and

Hildegard together, and they all followed Sven out into the wagon train. Sonja's paranoia began to flare up when Sven took the group towards the east, through the Hoademaker encampment.

"Isn't the Council wagon supposed to be near the center?" she asked.

"Yeah, but there was some problem with its wheels, so they brought the wagon to the handymen. Unfortunately the wagon is still with them," Sven replied.

It seemed like a reasonable answer, but something about it didn't feel right. Thankfully, she still felt the press of the knife against her leg. If anything happened she would be prepared.

***

Every important member stood outside the council wagon. The three important family members stood together: Yael Hoademaker leant on his cane, Rita Mattson stood up straight and glared at everyone, and because Gregor had died his son Sven joined them, looking a little in awe that he was now on their level. To the right of them, standing on his own, was the Administrator of the wagon train. He had long black hair that always shone greasily in the light, and had small eyes that made him look suspicious. Everyone knew him to be Hannes' puppet so no one gave him any respect, even Rita Mattson. To the left of the family leaders were Sonja and her friends, though there was a new girl that Sigrun didn't recognize, who looked a little shy and bookish. In Sigrun's experience you usually had to watch out for the shy types because they always surprised you with hidden passion.

All these people were here to vote on her new law. It felt strange that Sigrun stood amongst these important people. All she had been about a month ago was a lowly cattle rancher that had snuck into a party, and now she was creating laws and voting for them with other leaders. It was crazy, so much so that if she had been told it in one of her mother's fables she would have found it hard to believe.

Sigrun grinned, as she waited for the handymen to finish fixing back the Council wagon's wheels. She wanted to bask in this sense of leadership and power for some time, but she did have a job to do: to make sure the vote would go her way.

She strode up to Sven first, and asked him how he was doing after his father's funeral.

"It's hard, especially trying to take over everything that he controlled, but I'm getting there," he said.

"I know it was your father's wish to vote on this law, but what do you feel?"

Sven scratched his chin. "I'm a bit worried that a few farmers are still against it to be honest."

"I think that's to do with Hannes, but with this law in place he won't hold much sway over the farmers much longer," she said, keeping her voice low so Rita or the Administrator wouldn't hear.

"You might be right," Sven said, looking a little sad. "I feel I should uphold my father's wishes."

Sigrun patted him on the arm, and smiled. "You will do great, I believe in you."

Sven gave her a nod, but there was still something bothering him. She hoped that he could get through whatever it was and do what his father had wanted in the end.

But she couldn't control whether he did or not, so next went up to Yael. He stood next to Rita Mattson who glared even more when Sigrun walked up.

"You know this law is only hurting people," Rita said.

She felt it would be useless to try to argue the

case with her, so only said, "It's a mystery how you're going to vote." Instead she turned to Yael and asked him what he thought.

Yael glanced towards Rita. "I feel I might sit this vote out. There's too much bad blood between the families and I feel this is just going to cause more of it."

Sigrun wasn't totally surprised by that answer. Yael couldn't see the clear winning side with this law at the moment so would remain neutral. It was what the Hoademakers were known for after all.

Not wanting to ignore the faithful, she went over to them next.

It was a little awkward being with Sonja in front of others. She wanted to be closer to her, hold her hand, hug her, shout to the sky that they were in love, but instead she had to be at a respectful distance and give nothing away that they were together. It made her feel distanced from her, and a little lonely.

"Do you all like the new law?" she asked, trying to include all of them so she didn't have to act weird talking to Sonja.

The Priests and Priestesses next to Sonja nodded. They told Sigrun they really liked the harvest festival and wanted all parties to be more like that. The bookish girl looked surprised to be there and didn't really know how to answer the question. Sonja didn't answer, but looked suspiciously around the Council wagon.

"Are you still worrying about the attack?" Sigrun asked.

Sonja nodded. "There's something about this I don't like. I know nothing's happened to me yet, but that makes me more worried, not less."

"I know what you mean, but I've come prepared."

Sigrun had taken her own advice about protection and had wrapped a knife to her thigh, hidden underneath her trousers. If anyone wanted to attack her they would find a surprise stab to the face.

The handyman fixed the final wheel back onto the wagon. Sven walked up to the door and opened it, letting Yael and Rita go in first. Eventually they all filed their way into the wagon. Before Sigrun stepped in, she turned to Sonja and gave her a loving look. Sonja returned her own. Sigrun felt warmth within her heart. If anything happened she had one person she could rely on.

The inside of the council wagon was dominated

by a long and wide table, which had drawers set into it. In front of the drawers were cushioned chairs, five on each side of the table. Above these seats hung a representation for the two sides of the wagon train. On the faith's side there was a shining visage of Sol, on the workers side the three families' runes melded together to make one.

As each member of the Council took their seats, Sigrun stood at the front of the table. Her heart pounded. This was her moment, they would now vote for a law that she had brought in. She felt excited and nervous all at once. What if the vote didn't go her way?

"We have convened this Council in order to vote for a new law that will ban parties that are not officially sanctioned. After this law passes, the faithful and worker side's representatives will discuss how many parties there will be in a year and the provisions provided for those parties. The usual Council rules for a vote applies: a majority will bring the law in, a stalemate will mean the law doesn't pass but the law will be allowed to be voted on again in a months time, a majority against will defeat the law and it will not be allowed to be voted on again unless circumstances change significantly. Do you all understand these conditions?"

Everyone nodded around the table. Sigrun walked to her seat, and was about to begin the vote, but then she heard a whip crack. The wagon shuddered, and began to move.

The door burst open with a bang.

Hannes stepped in like he owned the place. He wore leather armor and wielded a sword. Behind him were many toughs also wielding swords. Sigrun recognized three of them straight away: the thin man Thore, the young farmer Daniel, and the thick armed Aina.

The toughs quickly stepped in and took the space behind each council member, there was one lackey for each of them. Aina stood behind Sigrun. The one that stood behind Sonja was the curly haired faithful who had talked with Hannes about the attack. So this was what they had been planning.

Hannes stood at the front of the table, looking as intimidating and powerful as possible. "Now there is going to be a slight change in what people are voting for today. Instead of the party law, you are going to vote Sigrun out as Jarl, and vote me in."

***

The weight of Britta's sword rested on Sonja's shoulder. There was a grim smile on Britta's lips. The smile let Sonja know that the friend that she had known all her life had gone. The woman behind her now was not Britta. Her friend would not gladly hold a sword to her neck and would have not joined in with a man that wanted to get rid of the faith. Sonja did not know who this new person was, or how the old Britta had become her, but she knew that she must be stopped, even if it meant stabbing her with a knife.

Hannes leant against the table, staring at them each in turn. There was satisfaction and malice in his eyes. He enjoyed this.

"Now, I want you all to vote," he said.

Rita, Yael, Sven, and the Administrator all put up their hands. Sigrun looked at them in surprise, especially at Sven. It looked like he had betrayed them as well.

Hannes shook his head. "I'm afraid that's just not good enough. I need to have a majority if I'm going to become Jarl."

"Why don't you kill us all now and be done with it?" Sigrun shouted.

"Because I need my power to seem legitimate to

the wagon train," he said as if he was talking to a child.

Sigrun snorted at that. "It'll never be legitimate, forcing people to vote with swords at their back."

Hannes waved that away. "No one will believe that, I'll make sure they won't. Now I feel I'm just going to have to persuade you to vote for me."

One of the thugs behind Sigrun, grabbed her shoulders and forced her to sit. Sonja cried out, but soon she had her own thug to contend with. Britta grabbed her by the neck with her arm, and squeezed.

Sonja coughed, and could feel pressure in her head. Britta grabbed hold of her hand, but Sonja pulled it away. She reached her hand towards her ankle, to grab the knife, but Britta pulled her back up.

The room began to swim, becoming fuzzy. She felt weak.

In front of her, Sigrun was having her own jostling match with her thug. Sigrun's face was contorted in a combination of worry and rage.

Eventually, Sigrun won out and wrestled free from her thug. There was a flash of metal and the thug cried out in pain. The surprise of what happened made Britta lose her grip, which allowed Sonja to breathe properly again. Not wasting the opportunity, she grabbed hold of her knife. She gripped the handle and plunged it into Britta's thigh, feeling satisfied when Britta stumbled backwards and whimpered in pain.

Both Sigrun and Sonja stood up, bloody knives in their hands. But their victory was short lived, as now they had all Hannes' goons stepped towards them, sword points straight in their face.

Hannes examined the two of them. "You are surrounded by people who will kill you if necessary. There is nowhere to go, we are at the edge of the wagon train. Now this can all be over, you can go back to your mundane lives for all I care, you just need to sit down and vote me in as Jarl."

Cold steel brushed Sonja's neck. She glanced around and saw three men and one woman ready to cut her down. She didn't feel there was a way out of this without either giving in or dying.

The thought of dying brought her back to that day when she had met Sigrun. Sigrun had saved her from stampeding cows. At that time it had been the sound of thunder and a lightning strike that had caused the stampede. She didn't have lightning but maybe if she caused her own thunder then the horses might bolt. She had seen some horses be skittish around loud noises.

Feeling like it was her only option to get out of this, she screamed as loud as she could and stamped her foot.

Someone at the front of the wagon shouted. The council wagon began to shudder and move forwards. Every thug glanced in each other's direction in worry. And then the world tipped over.

Sonja fell backwards in the air. A terrible cold suddenly hit her body. She shivered, and her teeth chattered. Her back hit the ground, hard enough that breath pushed out of her body.

She lay there for a few seconds, the wagon jostling and shaking around her. Sonja soon felt an icy burn at the ends of her fingers and at the corners of her ears. If she didn't move she would freeze to death.

She pushed herself up. A lot of attackers had been thrown on the floor, including Hannes. She grabbed one of their swords. It was hard keeping a grip because of the pain in her hands, and the constant shaking.

The horses whinnied. The wagon door waved in the cold wind. Sonja could see that the hill with the wagon train got further and further away. They had to get back, otherwise they would all freeze to death. The only question was how.

ONLY THE RAIDERS HAVE SURVIVED THE COLD OUTSIDE A SOL SHARD FOR A LONG TIME, BUT THEY FORCE THE LESSON FROM A YOUNG AGE

'Can We Survive Outside A Sol Shard?' by Tasgall Niven

Edven stood on Kveg Plain, watching his cows munch grass. In his hand was an orange rock that sparkled in the sunlight. Ever since receiving the rock from Sigrun - for butchering some of his livestock for the harvest festival - he liked to feel the hard crystalline surface and put it up to the light to see the brilliant glitter. He felt very happy about his trading choice, deciding that he'd probably keep the rock now instead of trading it for something else in town.

Movement caught the corner of his eye. A long and wide wagon trotted up through Kveg Plain. The wagon was made from posh dark wood, and the wheels looked like they had just been serviced. It definitely looked like the type of wagon that some of the important family members would live in, which made Edven curious. What made him more curious was how the wagon drove up to the edge of the Sol Shard's protection and parked itself there.

Edven had to know why someone had done such a strange thing, so he strode across the Plain to see what was happening. The door of the wagon was slightly ajar. He peered inside.

He saw glimpses of people in leather armor holding swords. In front of them were faces he recognized: Sigrun, Sven Baldur, and Yael Hoademaker. Sven and Yael sat at a table, worried expressions on their faces. Sigrun stood up, with every man and woman in leather armor pointing a sword at her. In her hand was a bloody knife.

Edven had no idea what was happening inside but he had to tell somebody about it. He turned around.

There was a loud scream. Horses whinnied, and hoofs hit the grass. The wagon's wheels creaked. Edven looked back. He saw the wagon barreling down the hill.

The wagon was now outside the Sol Shards protection. Everyone in that wagon would freeze to death if someone didn't save them. Edven ran as fast as he could into the wagon train.

***

The back of Sigrun's head hurt. The wagon around looked fuzzy. She could taste blood in her mouth, and could hear groans of others around her. She was also terribly cold. It was the kind of cold that stabbed right into your clothes and sucked out any warmth you thought you might have. She shivered. If she didn't get up she would freeze to death.

The wagon rattled and shook. At the front she could hear the constant pound of horses' hooves hit the ground. Glancing over to Sonja, who sported a very worried expression, confirmed her fear. They were moving, and they were moving further and further away from any protection against the deadly cold.

They had another problem. All around the wagon lay armored men and women, and they were slowly getting up. Next to them were their swords. If Sigrun didn't act fast they would surely grab hold of those swords, and the two of them would be in the same hostage situation they had been in before.

"Get the swords," she shouted to Sonja.

She bent to grab the sword she had stolen before. The thug on the floor saw what she was doing and grabbed at her leg. She swung the sword at his back. But because she didn't really want to kill him, and her fingers were shaking from the cold, the sword only scraped against the man's leather armor. The man grabbed her leg with the other arm and tried to pull her down. She pulled back and managed to get free, but then saw the man was grabbing hold of the sword's hilt.

Feeling like she had no choice, and apologizing – even though the man was probably willing to kill her – she swung the sword down, chopping the man's hand off.

The man screamed in pain, and blood spurted out onto the wooden floor. Sigrun looked away, feeling bile in her mouth. She coughed and spat it out. It was one thing to pretend to attack a man in the training yard, it was another thing to see the bloody effect of violence up close. She had never willingly caused pain to anyone before, and she didn't feel good about doing it.

But there was no time for those feelings, as she saw other thugs slowly push themselves off the floor and look for their swords. She breathed in and out, told herself that this was necessary, and strode towards the thugs.

She swung her sword at the grasping thugs. She slashed the shoulders of a woman, then stepped across and stabbed Thore in the hand. Unfortunately, when she made it to Aina, the woman had stood up and had a sword gripped in her hand.

But clearly the cold was getting to Aina, because she was shivering and shaking. Sigrun slashed her sword to the right. Aina managed to lift her sword up just in time, the clashing of metal ringing in the air. However Aina's grip wasn't strong enough, and her sword went flying out of her hands. Sigrun stepped towards her, ready to take her down, but Aina stepped back into the wall and put her hands up in surrender.

Sigrun stepped back, feeling a little ashamed that she had gotten so involved into the fight that she had been about to murder a defenseless woman. But just to be sure she wasn't stabbed in the back, she kicked Aina's sword out of the wagon.

Turning around, she saw that Sonja had been less forgiving than her. All the thugs on Sonja's side were now on the ground in pools of their own blood. Some of the blood was on Sonja's flame robe and dripped from her sword.

Sigrun was relieved that Sonja was ok, but a little disturbed that she had killed the thugs so readily. It made sense, Sonja had grown up in the faith which taught their Acolytes the art of killing your opponent, but it was still a shock to see someone that had done it so mercilessly. Sigrun couldn't deny that it scared her a little, and she thanked Sol that they were on the same side

The wagon was filled with bodies, either dead, in pain, or unconscious. The dead and in pain were mostly Hannes' thugs, and the unconscious were the heads of the families, the Administrator, and Sonja's friends. But Hannes was nowhere to be seen.

"Did you see him?" Sigrun asked.

"No, he must have gotten out of the door somehow," Sonja replied.

However, there was no time to see where he had run off to. The wagon still jostled and shook, and the two of them still shivered. They wouldn't have long to go before they froze to death.

"We need to stop this wagon," Sigrun said.

Sonja nodded, and they both stepped over bodies on the floor to get to the front of the wagon.

No one sat at the reins, which blew and flapped in the wind. The horses stampeded across the snow, going straight towards the river. Would the horses actually stop when they got to the river's edge, or would they just barrel right into the icy water, freezing everyone inside the wagon?

She took Sonja's hands, and squeezed it. They both sat down at the reins. The two of them looked at each other with love in their eyes. They nodded, counted to three, and pulled the reins as hard as they could.

The horses reared up, whinnied, and the whole front of the wagon rose up in the air and crashed back down, flinging both Sigrun and Sonja off into the snow.

***

Sonja found herself in a face full of snow. It tasted cold and wet. She pushed herself up, grabbing hold of her sword, and looked around to see where Sigrun had landed. It was not a good spot, some rocks jutted out of the snow.

She ran over to her, hoping that her beloved hadn't been killed. Sigrun didn't look good. She was splayed on the rock, unconscious. Her head was bleeding. Sonja gently shook Sigrun, hoping that she would wake up. But she didn't. For a second Sonja panicked, crying about how she didn't want Sigrun to die, but then felt breath under Sigrun's nose.

Sonja calmed down, breathing in deep. Everything would be alright if she was able to get back to the wagon train. But when she turned back towards their wagon her panic rose again.

The wagon had fallen on its side. The horses at the front stamped on the snow, trying to get free of their reins. It would take a team of six burly men to push the wagon back on its wheels.

Sonja felt defeated. She was on her own, she was miles out of the wagon train, she was exhausted from the fight and the panic, and she was freezing. In some way she just wanted to fall down onto the snow, and just sleep. Maybe then she would be able to go to the warm and loving paradise of Sol's resting place and enjoy its delights.

But she couldn't allow Sigrun and her friends to die as well. She steeled herself, and looked towards the wagon to see if there was anything she could do. The horses were only tied on by a rope, easily cut by a sword. She wouldn't be able to save everyone, but she might be able to get as many people as she could on the backs of those horses and ride them out. She had no idea how she would control two horses at once, but she would do her damnedest to try.

Thankfully the horse problem was solved for her, as Roose and Teresa crawled out of the back of the wagon. She rushed over to them and helped them up. The two of them looked a little blurry eyed and hurt, but they were able to stand and respond to her.

"I need you to help me put as many people on horses, and ride out towards the wagon train."

"What about you?" Roose asked.

"I need to keep whoever we don't save alive as long as possible, until we are rescued."

Teresa looked concerned. "You should take our place on the horse."

Sonja shook her head, her friends were more important than her. Even though she was the Keeper and pushed the path of the faith and kept them together, she would rather live, however briefly, in a world where they were alive than one without. "There's no time to argue either, we are all freezing to death. So go."

Roose and Teresa scrambled back into the wagon, while Sonja ran to the front. She carefully stepped towards one horse, putting a hand on its flank to soothe it. Then she walked to the rope and sawed it with her sword.

She ran over to where Sigrun lay, carefully picked her up – she was damn heavy – and put her unconscious body on the back of one of the horses. Sonja then ran to the back of the wagon and helped Roose and Teresa pull Yael Hoademaker's and Sven Baldur's unconscious body out, and onto the horses. It looked like there was room for one more, so they went back into the wagon and pull Sigmund's unconscious body out.

Roose and Teresa jumped on a horse each. They gave one last look to Sonja. She gave them a smile, and told them to ride as fast as possible. Even if this would be her final moments, she was glad to see them go.

The two of them kicked their horses, and rode out into the distance.

Sonja turned, and scrambled back into the wagon. A few unconscious people were starting to stir, but she ignored them. Instead, she went to the table and opened each drawer to see if there was anything useful within. Most of the drawers were filled with papers confirming the details of past laws and past votes, but she did find one drawer which had some orange rock dust and some matches.

The orange rocks were not only an excellent trading resource, but they also burned very easily. Feeling lucky, she took the drawer out and sprinkled the orange dust around the table. But before she put it alight, she needed to get everyone out of the wagon.

She ran on adrenaline, but the cold was still cutting through. Her fingers had become numb, and she was starting to feel a little woozy and sleepy. She staggered sometimes when she tried to drag out a body, and felt an overwhelming feeling of just wanting to give up and lie down.

Sonja refused to do so, shaking her head, and sometimes slapping herself. She dragged each body that wasn't dead or dying out. Some, like Rita and Hildegard, had woken up enough that they were able to crawl out of the wagon themselves.

She came across Britta's body, and checked to see if she was alive. She was. Should she save her former friend? Britta had been a part of this attack and had been willing to strangle Sonja to get what she wanted. Sonja could so easily leave her here to die and no one would think she had done it deliberately. Britta would just be another thug that had died in the attack.

But Sonja couldn't leave her there. The Britta unconscious on the floor might not be the Britta she knew, but they still had a history together. Sonja still felt some kind of bond with her former friend. She grabbed Britta's body and dragged her out of the snow.

When everyone was out, she lit the match and threw it at the rocks. She crawled away from the ensuing blaze as fast as possible.

The wagon quickly burned. The heat of the fire was a welcome relief from the cold, and Sonja tried to get her and the unconscious bodies as close to the flames as possible. She sat down next to Rita and Hildegard, seeing the flames rise up and the smoke fill the sky.

She had done as much as she could, now the rest was up to the wagon train.

Sonja didn't have to wait long. As the wagon in front turned into a blazing bonfire, she heard the pound of hooves and the squeak of wheels. Several wagons rode out towards her group, many wagons were driven by men and women in yellow robes. Her own faithful were here to save them.

She felt joy in her heart as her Priestesses and Priests jumped down, grabbed hold of Yael, Rita, Sven, Britta, and the rest, and dragged them inside. She didn't need to be dragged, she pushed herself up, and walked into a wagon. Inside was the familiar face of the old farmer with the mustache that had given the faithful his meat.

Sonja was surprised to see him, but grateful that he had a part to play in their rescue. She nodded to him, but as soon as she sat down all the adrenaline that had rushed through her body dissipated. Her head drooped, and her eyes closed.

THE ACT OF UNION WASN'T JUST FOR ME AND SIGRUN, IT WAS FOR THE WHOLE OF THE WAGON TRAIN

'Scroll of Keeper Sonja'

Sigrun opened her eyes. Her head throbbed, hurting a lot more than any past hangover. However she did feel warm again, and her surroundings, even though they were slightly blurred at the moment, looked a lot like the inside of a wagon.

How had she made it back into the wagon train? All she remembered was flying off the wagon and rocks coming towards her, everything after that had been black.

She sat up, feeling a sharp pain in her head. A hand gripped hers, and she heard a voice say, "You don't have to get up."

Sigrun turned, and saw a figure sitting next to her bed. It took awhile for her vision to clear to recognize it was Sonja. Sonja had a mixture of concern and relief in her face, but her eyes had a toughness to them that Sigrun had never seen before.

"What happened?" Sigrun asked.

Sonja snorted, and shook her head. "Too much, but it's all good now. Everyone was saved."

"Did anyone find Hannes?" she asked.

"Yes we did eventually, he had been running in the snow for an hour before being picked up by the people who saved us. Him, Britta, the Administrator, and the three Elders are tied up in one of the faith's wagons, and are being guarded."

Sigrun was surprised the Elders had been tied up. "Won't they be really pissed about that?"

"Well they should have thought about that when they allowed Hannes to attack us," Sonja said, bitterly.

Sigrun felt like her head hurt too much, because she didn't see the connection between the Elders and Hannes. "I don't think there is any evidence to tie them with what Hannes did, maybe Rita and the Administrator, but not Yael and Sven."

Sonja sighed. "They were all in on it. Don't you think they were a little quick on voting you out?"

"They did have people pointing swords at them."

"And yet us faithful didn't put our hands up, you didn't."

"Yeah, but I've always been stupid," she said,

trying to push herself up and getting a stabbing pain in her head again. "And you faithful have more experience in situations involving violence."

"I guess I can't prove it, which means they'll probably be released eventually," Sonja said, shaking her head. "But you really shouldn't trust those people anymore."

Sonja might be right. She would have never trusted Rita, but Yael also seemed suspect. The wagon had been brought over to the handymen, which lived in the Hoademakers encampment. This had allowed Hannes and the rest to get close without any suspicion. But did that mean Yael had been in on it?

Sigrun had also been surprised when Sven put up his hand to vote her out. If she confronted him he was sure to explain it. He would say that he was scared of the thugs, but that felt a little hollow to her. In her mind you should never bow to anyone who used violence to get you to do something, they'll only use it again on you later. Also she felt that the thugs would have never killed someone like Sven.

Thinking about whether she could trust the people around her made her wish she could be back being a cattle rancher, looking after cows.

They never turned on you for more power.

"I don't really know what I'm going to do if you are right. I may be the Jarl, but my power does come from them," she said, tired of having to think about politics. All she wanted to do was cuddle up to Sonja and forget everything.

"From what I understand the power of the Jarl is absolute, so you can change things if you want," Sonja said.

"But significant changes, like new laws and power arrangements, need to be agreed by the Council. I believe, from what you told me, most of the Council is now tied up so won't be able to vote for some time."

"Yeah they're tied up, and suspicion is on them about an attack on our lives. That should mean they don't get a say anymore," Sonja said, leaning towards her. "Think about it, what if we decide on everything? What if we become the new Council, deciding what happens and enacting it ourselves? It's clear we care more about the people, both sides of them, than they do.

It did sound appealing to Sigrun, understanding what people wanted and enacting it themselves. They wouldn't have to persuade the Elders and other Council members it was in their best interests to vote for it. They would just think of something and it would be done. But there was one big flaw.

"What if we disagree like we did about the future of the wagon train?"

"We discuss it and try to find a compromise," Sonja said.

"What if we are both passionate about something that it blinds us, or makes us go on the defensive?"

Sonja rubbed her chin. "Good point, maybe on those occasions we get a third party that we can both agree on to find a compromise or suggest something different for us."

"And what about the important families? They do a lot of important jobs for the wagon train, they are going to want some power because of that."

"They have power over their own people. But those people have a voice as well, and we will listen to it. Sometimes they might be lucky and their desires and the people's will align, but sometimes they won't and they will have to lump it or find some other wagon train."

Sigrun was taken aback by Sonja's hard words. The incident in the Council Wagon had definitely sharpened her. But she did like what she was saying. She had just had a very frustrating experience trying to persuade the Council on her new law and because of Hannes it had ever even been enacted.

"I'm in."

***

Sonja spent a lot of time next to Sigrun's bed while Sigrun was recovering. She didn't for one second go out of Sigmund's wagon, deciding to sleep in the chair. Usually, the two of them slept with their hands intertwined. It comforted Sonja to know Sigrun was next to her, and that she was there to keep her safe.

This did mean that Sigmund was the first one to know about her secret, but after all that she had been through Sonja didn't really care.

Sigmund told her a crowd had gathered outside his wagon every day, and the crowd didn't just contain faithful. He talked about how farmers, weavers, butchers, and faithful all talked to one another, waiting for any sign of two of them. Sonja found that a little strange, but also touching. She hadn't really thought the whole wagon train would really care about how they were after what had happened. She told Sigmund that she would only step outside when Sigrun had fully recovered.

Thankfully, Sigrun did recover. At first it was just sitting up without too much pain, but then she was able to get out of bed and walk around. There were a few occasions where she fell, and Sonja had to catch her, but these became less and less frequent. Eventually, Sigrun said that she was sick of the sight of the wagon and wanted to go out.

"I'll warn you, there are a lot of people waiting for us outside," Sonja said.

"Are they here to praise us, or throw rotten lettuce?" Sigrun asked.

"Praise us, I believe."

Sigrun grinned. "Well we shouldn't let them wait too long."

Despite being forewarned, Sonja was still surprised by the amount of people in the crowd. The whole faith encampment was filled with what looked like every single person in the wagon train. They all cheered when they stepped out.

Sigrun waved at them, looking like she was overjoyed at the reception. Sonja couldn't help but feel joy as well. The two of them were alive, and ready to lead the wagon train.

Sonja couldn't think of another person she would rather want to be with now.

Even though the crowd of faithful were watching and they didn't know her secret, she threw caution to the wind and grabbed hold of Sigrun's hand. Sigrun turned, surprised.

Sonja didn't wait. It was like the same spirit that had possessed her when she had been saved by the stampeding cows was possessing her now. She leaned forwards and kissed Sigrun.

There were gasps from the faithful section of the crowd, but Sonja didn't care. This felt right, this was who she was and who she would be from now on. If the faith didn't like that they didn't deserve her.

However, most in the crowd cheered again and shouted out in joy. She turned to them and smiled. Everything was what she had wanted.

She turned, and saw Sigrun grin. Sigrun clasped both Sonja's hands so they were intertwined. The crowd gasped again, this was a gesture that only meant one thing.

"Sonja," Sigrun said, as loud as possible so the crowd could hear. "Will you join me in union?"

Tears streamed down Sonja's cheeks. She opened her mouth, but choked. She had to close her eyes, breathe in a little, and open her eyes again. "Yes, I would."

Sigrun grinned again, and kissed her. It was a kiss of passion, as if the crowd were not staring at them.

The act of union was in some ways unlike Sonja's vision. The wagon wasn't divided in the middle and no one wielded swords. But in some ways it was exactly like her vision. She dressed in white, while her friends wore bright orange. They held bunches of flowers, which they threw in the gathered crowd while they walked past.

Everyone in the wagon train had packed themselves in the faith's encampment, which made it hard for Sonja and her friends to get through.

Sonja felt the overwhelming joy of the crowd, which buoyed her and made her heart sing. Though there were a few spots that dampened the spirit down. Some faithful looked on at her, aghast; and Hannes and Britta stood in their little prison wagon, watching the proceedings with horror.

She ignored them, and focused on the joy. She

pushed her way through to the crowd to the Keeper's podium. Sigrun stood at the top. Her beauty caught Sonja's breath. Sigrun's face and hair shone as brightly as the white dress she wore. Her intricate knotted braid added some formality to her, but her easy grin showed the messy confidence underneath.

Sonja's heart leapt with joy with every step to the podium. This felt right. The two of them were coming together, and so was most of the wagon train. She stood in front of Sigrun, staring deep in her eyes.

Sigmund ran the ceremony, which involved saying vows and confirming their union. As Sonja said each one she felt as if a chain with the name Sigrun engraved in it was binding across her heart. She did not want to be free. When the final vow was said, Sigmund told them that they could kiss.

It might have been her imagination, but as they did Sonja saw a bright light pulsating out. It hit the crowd and blinded them. She knew instantly it was the light of Sol. The goddess was giving the union her blessing. Sonja felt even more comforted and loved.

Just like her vision, after the kiss her and

Sigrun turned to the crowd. They put up their hands, and said in unison, "We will lead you now."

Free Book!

How Manang Ate The Sun and Other Fables
J.A. Day

Want to know more about Sigrun's past and some of her favorite fables? Learn how the world became an icy wasteland, how Sigrun got her braid, the real story behind her father's death, and the fable that inspired her to stop being a cattle rancher and start being someone important. Read all this in *How Manang Ate The Sun, and Other Fables*. To get this book sign up to my newsletter at: jadaybooks.com/newsletter

Thank You!

Thank you so much for purchasing this book and reading to the end of it. It means so much to me that the ideas and characters I created are out there and being read by people like you. I hope you enjoyed it.

Independent authors like me need the help of readers like you to be noticed in the sea of content out there. It would mean a lot if you went to the place you bought the book and reviewed it. Don't worry you don't have to write an essay, just say if you liked it or not and give it a star rating. It really helps. And hey, if you really loved this book maybe even recommend it to someone you know.

If you want to keep up to date on the books I have please go to my website: jadaybooks.com

If you want to get updates of when new books are going to get released please like my Facebook page: www.facebook.com/JDXercies. It is also a place where I will share the Fantasy books I'm reading and the activities I'm doing.

If you are interested in following what's happening with me on a more casual basis, you can follow me on Twitter: twitter.com/JDXercies.

Last but not least, if you really loved the cover design of this book and the free book please follow my cover designer, Meli, on Instagram: instagram.com/meliplanet

Acknowledgments

First of all, thank you so much to the wonderful partner I had for ten years, Emily Perugia, who sadly passed away before they could read this novel. Without their love, their pushing of me to always do my best, and the emotional grounding of a happy home, I wouldn't be confident or happy enough to write or publish this book. You are terribly missed every day and I will always cherish the joy and silliness you brought into my life.

Thank you to Selristai, Elisterre, and the others at the Loaded Trifle discord writing group. Without your short story competitions, and very brutal but necessary critiques, I wouldn't have become a good writer. You picked up all the problems I had with my work and gave me the very necessary tools to improve. You also taught me what common rules of writing that I probably shouldn't follow. I owe a lot to all of you and hope to see some of your books out there on the shelves. Double thanks to Selristai for editing this book and making it that much better.

Thank you to my family: Mum and Dad, Dahnya, Phillip and his wife Kerry, Robert and his wife Kerri(yeah it confuses us as well), Andrew, John, and Helen, for giving me emotional support, reading the book, and giving advice. Also you know, for raising me and encouraging my pursuit of the creative arts. Thank you to my siblings for all the engaging arguments about games and books over the years.

Thank you to my friends, Adam Taylor and Jo MacQueen, who I had a lot of fun working and making films with back in the day, and would always find my discussions about what I'm writing entertaining. They also encouraged my creativity a lot.

Thank you to the members of the Dice Club: Adam, Simon, Bexy, JD, Martin, and Meli for being a great gaming and friend group. You made life a lot more entertaining and funny, especially during a sadder time in my life. Special thanks obviously goes to Meli for being a great cover designer, and making this book look beautiful.

About The Author - James Anthony Day

When I was 10 years old I found a copy of Fellowship Of The Ring in my school's library. The story of hobbits going on a journey through Middle earth, and singing while doing it, created a life time of passion for the Fantasy genre. The film that came out a year later sealed the deal.

I've always written from a young age, creating stories about zombies when I was a child – I got in trouble with the teacher because they were too gory – and creating stories about space battles and robots when I was a teenager. But they never came to anything. I was one of those writers that would write a chapter and then go onto the next thing, always bursting with ideas but never completing them.

I started to take writing more seriously in late 2016. I had just moved to a new job in London and felt like I had a lot of free time in the evenings, and it was coming to NaNoWriMo. Feeling like I missed writing stories and I had never completed one, I decided to join the competition. The first story was terrible, but the feeling of finishing was incredible. This started a journey of trying to get better at the craft of writing, and trying to get the fantastical ideas in my head on paper.

Apart from writing, in my free time I like to play Roleplaying Games. My brother introduced me when I was younger, but it wasn't until university when playing with friends did I truly get into it. I started as a Game Master straight away because everyone wanted to play an RPG but no one wanted to run it.

It was trial by fire, having to learn how to make narrative and get rules right on the fly. But I loved the experience. The ability of creating my own worlds, acting out characters, and creating intriguing situations for my players to deal with was exciting.

At the moment I live in London, and I work as a health administrator for the NHS. In my spare time I play board games with a local group on Wednesday evenings, and am currently looking to GM an RPG soon.

Printed in Great Britain
by Amazon